A DAY WITHOUT A NIGHT

DARK AS NIGHT TRILOGY #2

JT ADELINE

For my son Travis, whose endless amounts of energy helped to set the pace of my characters.

And for my niece Gabby, because Dracula had to have a sunburn.

THE GUSTAVO FAMILY TREE

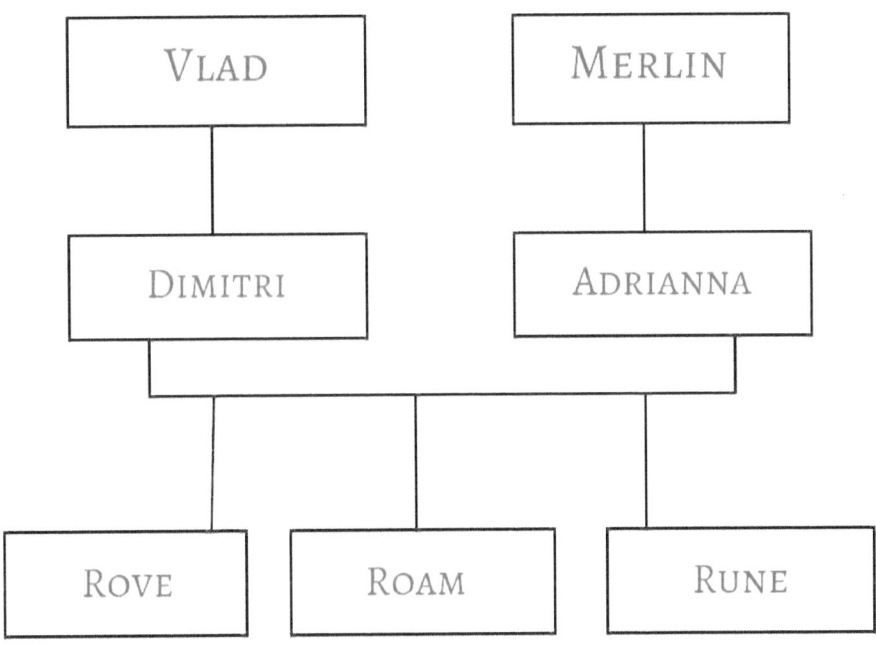

VLAD

MERLIN

DIMITRI

ADRIANNA

ROVE

ROAM

RUNE

1

Dust and dirt kicked up in the fading light as Rune Gustavo entered the cave four miles from his home in Pyatt Township in the center of Minnesota. He ran his fingers along the sides of the roughly carved walls, willing a star orb into his other hand. Just over a month ago, he and his identical brothers, along with their best friend, Maya Stewart, had received powers from a prophecy written well before any of them had even been born. They had been chosen to stop immortality for over five hundred, rogue, nightwalker vampires who were going insane and infecting others. It felt good to save mankind.

He stepped into the doorway at the center of the cave and smiled, remembering he made this new doorway. This was where their first fight had begun with an evil sorceress who was helping the rogue vampires. The sorceress, Kya, had quickly discovered she was no match to any of their powers and was now being held by their grandfather, Merlin the Wizard, in some magical realm.

Still testing out the parameters of his power, Rune willed the orb in his upturned hand to grow larger and was pleased when it illuminated far into the cavernous space. Why was he here? What was he here to find? Turning in a circle Rune sent out feelers to make sure there wasn't a threat hiding somewhere within the cave, something that he had been able to do for as long as he could remember. He could still feel the pull he had felt when he flew overhead only a half hour before. Only now, it felt more like a tethered connection not wanting to let loose and he believed he had no other choice but to find out why.

Rune turned more slowly when his orb illuminated the cave art they had all made when they were ten. He recognized the spot where Maya had fallen and cut open her chin, and smiled when he saw the space where he hid food in case they ever were trapped inside. Finishing his circle, he stopped when he saw broken furniture spewed across the cave floor, and something glimmering in the light his orb made mere inches from a broken tabletop along the far wall.

The crunching under his shoes was loud in the silence as he made his way to whatever he had seen. He lowered the orb to see broken glass, and what appeared to be crushed ceramic. It was spread across the floor in varying sizes and colors as if others had done the same as him, grinding the glass into the earthen floor. The pull was stronger now, making it feel as if the cave floor was pulsating under his feet. He stepped over a broken table leg and the remains of a chair, until he found what might have been shining under the light of his orb.

Crouching down Rune picked up what appeared to be a washer on a long, broken silver chain. He rolled the washer between his fingers noticing a difference. It had been made flat like the new jewelry Maya bought with inspirational words stamped on it, and in its center was what appeared to be a flattened piece of copper with something imprinted there.

"Hey, Rune? You go to Transylvania for those Oreos or what? The love of your life is here."

Rune snickered, continuing to roll the washer between his fingers, shaking his head, and listening to his oldest brother, Rove's telepathic message. Rune and his brothers were identical—triplets—and the last of the Gustavo vampires who were directly related to Dracula. Being vampires, they were able to communicate with each other telepathically, as long as they weren't more than ten miles away from each other. They could also tap into another vampire's thoughts, if the other wasn't blocking.

Running his fingers across the dirt, Rune realized the pull had stopped. But why? He looked at the compressed washer in his hand. Was this what he was meant to find? What was so special about an inexpensive necklace? Not having an answer, he stood, sticking the necklace into the front pocket of his jeans.

"Rune! Where the heck are you?"

"I'm coming," Rune answered silently, lifting the orb to see more of the area. *"Don't get your undies in a bunch."* He slowly walked back to the entrance, sweeping his orb from left to right. Nothing else stood out or called to him, nothing made him feel as if he needed to stay. He extinguished the orb and repositioned his backpack, filled with Merlin and Dracula's favorite cookies, his mind wandering. If he was meant to find the necklace, what was its significance? If it had magical properties, wouldn't it have sparked or glowed when he had touched it? He shook his head, placing his hands on his hips while stepping out into the evening sun. The rays touching his exposed skin still felt warm and comforting. Being early June, he was grateful it wasn't blistering hot. One never knew what the weather would do in Minnesota.

Taking a deep breath, Rune shot from the ground, pushing off with his feet and drawing his arms tight against his sides. He let the adrenaline pulsate through his body as he shot past the trunks of trees, and their treetops. He skimmed his fingers along the tallest branches and their soft green leaves. He flew over the dense forest, traveling in a circle making a wide arc before heading towards home.

Rune and his brothers were Daywalker vampires. Over time, vampires had evolved to make a new breed that could walk the day and the night, eat food, appear human, and have a life span as long as any human being could. Dracula and the vampires who walked only the night were Nightwalker vampires. Nightwalkers had more power, much like how superheroes were portrayed, their eye color was black making it appear as if their pupils had overtaken their eyes, and they were immortal. Until recently, nightwalkers were still only able to survive on blood, but since Dracula and his followers had helped in fighting the rogue vampires, the Sorceress of the Sun gave only them the ability to eat food and enjoy sunlight once again.

Rune loved to be in the open air and flying, as if nothing else in the world mattered. He very rarely had the opportunity to spend time alone, being a triplet, and wanted to relish in the silence, to only do what he wanted, even if it was for only ten minutes more. But he had taken too much time already and needed to get home to where his family and friends celebrated the triplet Gustavo brothers' graduation, and now Teagan was there. Rune smiled recalling Rove's message of her arrival and stopped, hovering above the treetops looking to where his home sat a quarter of a mile ahead. Being a vampire he was able to see for miles, hear things from miles away and feel more pain that not only belonged to him, but his brothers as well.

He brought his home into focus, looking between all who gathered there. He watched as his mom laughed at something his Uncle Radek was saying, then his dad as he came up behind his wife and encircled his arms around her waist.

Then, there she was. All five feet to his six walking between the tables with her friends, Posh and Diego. Her copper hair was cut short, spiking out in every direction, to show off a strong jaw and high cheekbones. He couldn't help but notice the blue jean Capris she wore, folded up below her knees with blingy jewels on the back pockets. Her blue canvas tennis shoes matched her button down blue shirt that was knotted in front, to show off a pierced belly button. When he saw her smile, his mouth went dry, and when she turned just slightly he could see her amber eyes making his heart beat faster.

Teagan was the most beautiful girl he had ever seen, and he couldn't speak a coherent sentence when she was around. He knew his cheeks grew red when she looked anywhere in his direction. Whenever she spoke, he just wanted to melt into every word she said with her musical Irish lilt. And when she threatened to beat the crap out of him or his brothers whenever they did anything annoying, he wanted to wrap her up in his arms and never let go. Rune sighed, taking one last long look at Teagan before leaving the branches behind to fly once more. How could he have Teagan for a girlfriend? If he couldn't speak around her, how was he supposed to ask her out?

TEAGAN FINNEGAN WEAVED her way around the tables set up in the Gustavo backyard, nodding at those who greeted her as she passed. She hadn't wanted to come, though she liked Maya and the Gustavo boys just fine, especially Rune. He was cute and sweet and he made her laugh, but... she didn't feel as if she belonged. They had powers she could only dream about, something she would never have. She dragged her feet for as long as she could, until Posh and Diego had literally grabbed her from the house they were currently staying at. They had landed ten minutes ago.

"Relax, Teagan," Vlad said telepathically. *"You look as if you want to chomp down on someone's neck and feast."*

Teagan looked over at Vlad's smiling face and sneered. He was sitting at a table with Radek and Francesca, a mound of food in front of him. Even sitting one could tell he was an intimidating man. Six foot four, a muscular body and raven black hair that hung straight past his shoulders. He wasn't called 'Vlad the Impaler' for nothing, and no other undead vampire was stronger than he was.

"Maybe it will be your neck I feast on," she answered silently, as she smiled sweetly and gave a curtsy.

"And only you can get away with saying something like that," Posh said from next to her as Vlad laughed.

Teagan winced. When you lived and traveled with a number of vampires, your thoughts were their thoughts unless you put up blocks to only speak with one or certain ones. It wasn't difficult to do, once you learned how to do it. It just took a certain amount of concentration, something Teagan was usually without.

"He's much more relaxed since meeting his grandsons," Teagan answered aloud. She followed Posh to the food table, picking up a paper plate and popping a purple grape into her mouth. "He has more of a reason to live out his life now."

Posh turned, looking down to face her. Her long single braid draped over one shoulder, a shocked expression on her beautiful face, *"You* gave him a reason to live out his life, Teagan. He loves you as if you were his own."

Teagan grabbed a ham sandwich and a handful of chips, dropping them on her plate alongside the grapes. "I'm nobody special, Posh. I didn't ask to be his favorite any more than being parentless." She abruptly left the table, not wanting to get into the discussion of her parents and how much she missed them.

"Posh was only trying to calm your nerves, Teagan," Vlad said in her mind as she made her way to his table. She placed her plate on the end and stood beside the one who gave her a home and a family. Vlad reached over, placing a strong hand on top of her small one. She looked over into his black pleading eyes as she stuffed a chip into her mouth, shaking her head slightly.

"I'll go and apologize," she said with a huff. "But don't expect me to hug her."

Vlad patted her hand before she picked up her plate and walked to the other end of the table to join Posh. She took a moment to look in his direction and stick her tongue out. Sometimes Dracula could be so annoying.

"When you are done eating, go and find the boys and Maya," Vlad said, laughing. *"And stop being a brat. Don't make me ground you."*

"Sure thing, Master." Teagan gave Vlad a more sincere smile just before putting a block on her thoughts. Everything had been fine until they had come here to help the Gustavos. Now, Vlad seemed to have some sort of plan where she was concerned, wanting her to hang with kids her own age instead of the adults. Maybe she liked hanging with the adults. They didn't seem to do stupid things. Well, not usually.

2

As Rune's feet gently touched the ground, he removed the pack from his back and grasped it in his fingers. He smiled at family and friends making his way to his mom, handing off his bag.

"Five packages of Oreos, each a different flavor as ordered."

"Thank you, Rune." His mom looked at him, leaning her head slightly to one side. "What's wrong?"

He smiled. "Nothing. It's a good night to fly, that's all. Where's Roam and Rove?"

Mom gave him *the look*. The one that meant she didn't believe anything he just said. "In the tree house with Maya, they want you to join them."

"Thanks." Rune went to leave but turned back when his mom's hand lightly touched his arm.

"Teagan's here."

"I know." He took his mom's hand in his, giving it a squeeze while he smiled. He could feel his mom's eyes on his back as he walked away. He paused for a moment, wanting to turn back, to talk with his mom about how he was feeling and ask her opinion on how to fix his unease when he was around Teagan. Instead, he shrugged off the feeling of prying eyes, swiped a graduation cupcake from the table, and made his way to the wooden ladder, which led to the inside of the tree house, beginning to climb.

The tree house had been built in a very large, old, oak tree, which no longer produced leaves, just inside the woods in their yard. As it grew, it seemed to grow outward, leaving a gap at its center as if asking for a house to be put into its branches. Old Man Philip, whose cabin stood empty in the middle of the dense forest, which bordered their house, had taken down a small barn on his property and had offered them the wood to make a tree house. So Rune, his brothers, and their dad went to work. It was larger than the average tree house, tall enough for an adult to stand in and roomy enough for his entire family.

"Alright, I'm here," Rune said, tossing his last bite of cupcake into his mouth, clearing the ladder. "What's the emergency?"

Maya stood from the square picnic table where his brothers Roam and Rove were still sitting, motioning for Rune to take a seat. He straddled one of the vacant stools while flicking hair out of his eyes and raising an eyebrow at Maya. He was still getting used to the purple streaks in her blonde shoulder length hair, compliments from the prophecy. It had all started with a book. And that was exactly what was plopped into his lap by Maya.

"What's this, a graduation gift for me?" he asked picking up the unfamiliar book with an intricate design of a sun on the cover. It was no bigger than a standard hardcover book and just as thick.

"The book left for me by my birth mother, Brea, the Sorceress of the Sun."

Rune jumped to his feet, holding the book in his hands away from his body as if it were a bomb ready to explode. He gingerly set it on the picnic table and backed away. "No way! Nuh-uh! I am not opening another book! Get rid of it!" He backed up to the doorway, placing his hand on the top rung of the ladder.

"Oh, come on Rune. How bad can it be?" Maya picked up the book, holding it against her chest as she looked over at him with her dark brown eyes.

"Don't you mean to say how bad *can it* get?" he answered, taking a firm grip on the top rung. "And this from the one who actually died and was brought back by a sorceress," he added under his breath but loud enough for all to hear. The prophecy had stated Rune and his brothers would end immortality once they had linked with a fourth with unknown powers. Maya had turned out to be the fourth. She had sacrificed herself to fulfill the prophecy, and was brought back by Brea, the Sorceress of the Sun, she later found to be her birth mother.

"Why should we care if it is bad or not?" Rove said, leaning back against the wall, his arms crossed over his chest showing his ever-present attitude. "We received great gifts from fulfilling the prophecy that no one else in the world possesses." He flicked his wrist making one of his red, dragon scaled ropes of magic appear which could be put to flame on a whim.

"Don't you have any adventure left in you, Rune?" Roam asked while taking the book from Maya and setting it on his lap. He placed his hand on the cover and looked up at Rune.

Rune pointed a finger at his brother. "Don't do it, Roam! Don't open it!"

"What's with you anyway?" Roam asked through raven bangs streaked with blue that were always in his eyes. "I thought you got a kick out of fulfilling the prophecy?"

"Okay, maybe I am overreacting just a little bit." Rune indicated with his ring finger and thumb how little he thought he was overreacting. "But seriously, we almost didn't make it through the last ordeal. I'm not sure if I want to try another so soon."

"It's just a book." Maya placed her hand in Roam's hair beginning to toy with it, while he grabbed her other hand bringing her down for a quick kiss. "I'm sure it only has information on my birth mother and her family. Why would she give me something that could harm us?"

"Have you looked at it yet?" Rune took a few steps back towards them.

"No. I decided we should look at it together."

"Like last time." Rune dragged his hands through his hair remembering what happened the last time they opened a book.

"I seem to recall it was you who found the last book," Rove said, pushing away from the wall. The red streaks in his hair became more evident as he leaned forward under the bulb in the ceiling. "We just had to go and look at it." He put up two fingers on each hand to emphasize with quotation marks.

"Exactly my reason for not opening that book. I'm telling you it's not a good idea." Rune moved to stand beside Rove pointing down at the book in question still in Roam's lap. "I just don't have a good feeling about this."

"You having your bad mojo vibes?" Rove asked, referring to Rune's ability to sense danger.

"Not exactly," Rune answered, shifting nervously from foot to foot. "Just uneasy."

"Well, I don't." Maya reached down and flipped open the cover of the book. "See, there is nothing..."

"Close it!" Rune yelled, but he didn't feel the threat until it was already too late, something he normally was able to feel way before it was near.

From out of the book came black light which hit the wall of the tree house directly behind Maya, making the four of them jump back. Rune grabbed Maya, pulling her away from the blackness while he and his brothers revealed their fangs, the color of their eyes turning red. Rove flicked both wrists bringing out two red ropes, snapping them to bring them to flame, while the others brought out what was given to them. Maya shot out her purple barrier, trying to ward off whatever had come out of the book while Roam's hands began to spark blue lightning, ready to use if needed. Rune had two orbs of white stars capable of exploding on impact in each hand, one he began to toss in the air, his eyes on the black light on the wall.

Faces began to appear on the blackness, like those in a black and white silent movie. Rune watched as something silver flashed across the screen and just as suddenly a figure appeared in the frame, bound and gagged to a chair. As Maya dropped her barrier, the Gustavo brothers stared into the eyes of their grandfather Pappy, Merlin the Wizard.

Pappy's eyes were nearly swollen shut, a bruise over the bridge of his nose, his long usually white beard, and hair looking mangy. Even with his evident injuries, he sat up tall almost with an air of confidence as something silver flashed in front of Pappy's face to be held under his chin. Rune's blood turned cold when Riebl, their archenemy, taunted them from the inky blackness. As they continued to watch, it appeared as if a camera were moving backward as yet another person appeared in its frame. Kya, the sorceress whom they had captured along with a handful of daywalker vampires, smiled eerily at them from the black wall.

"My dear chosen ones," she sneered, her long, thick, red hair curling perfectly around a beautiful face. "You have until a day without a night to bring me the book of Light and Dark, and the key. You bring them to me and I will spare the all-powerful Merlin. You fail to do as I ask," she smiled at them from the blackness so only her face showed, "not only will I kill your beloved Pappy, but I will take all of your powers. All of them!" Kya stepped back, visibly composed herself, running her hands down her long flowing emerald gown.

"The book you have opened will aid you in finding the key, and help lead you to the place where you will bring me both the key and the book. I strongly advise you to heed my words. I'll be waiting for you. Good luck." The blackness began to expand until it exploded knocking all four of them on their backsides.

"You were saying?" Rune said, rubbing his back where it hit the wall.

"Why is it we keep getting knocked off our feet by that woman?" Rove protested through gritted teeth, picking himself up from off the floor, offering a hand to Roam.

"I thought Riebl was dead?" Roam said loudly. "That he perished along with the other nightwalkers when Maya fulfilled the prophecy!"

"I must have forgotten to tell you," Maya said as she slowly sat up. "I saw Riebl take to the sky just moments before I destroyed the rest of them." Rune saw her wince as she touched the back of her left arm. Her fingers came back coated with blood. "I'm sorry. I should have listened to you, Rune."

Roam knelt down in front of her. "You didn't know any of this would happen," he said, carefully looking at her arm, and then drawing her eyes to his. "None of us did."

"How bad is it?" Rune asked looking over Roam's shoulder.

"Bad enough that Mom will need to take a look at it."

"Well, one good thing could happen from yet another adventure," Rove said, staring at Maya's arm.

"Which is?" Rune asked, not sure he wanted to hear the answer.

"Maybe one of us will get the power to heal."

COLORS GLOWED and danced across the windows of the tree house, drawing Teagan's attention, just before she heard what sounded like a small explosion. She was on her feet and running long before anyone else knew where the sound had come from.

"Please be okay, please be okay," she murmured as she moved with vampiric speed, making the air snap, as she defied gravity and materialized inside the tree house. Relief poured through her as she saw Rune with his white streaks in his raven hair, alive, well, and unharmed.

"Everyone okay?" she asked, looking to each one, trying to show indifference. Her eyes stopped at Rune in his snug fitting blue jeans and white t-shirt. With difficulty, she turned her eyes away. Several more snaps popped the air around her as first Dimitri with Adrianna appeared, followed closely by Radek and Vlad. Posh and Diego filled the doorway as Teagan was pushed aside so the boys' parents could get to Maya still sitting on the floor, holding the back of her left arm.

"What happened?" Dimitri asked, his raven black, shoulder length hair falling across his face and into his deep blue eyes, just like his sons. He knelt in front of Maya and took her arm in his hands, carefully pulling up her shirtsleeve so Adrianna could look underneath.

"Psycho freak sorceress and her nightwalker puppet have Pappy," Rune answered, his cheeks turning a light pink when he gazed toward Teagan.

"How?" Adrianna's green eyes held a question as she looked up at her son while gently helping Maya to her feet. "Rune, how? How do you know this?"

"Ahh," Rune began as Rove slapped him in the arm. "Out of the book," he stammered, digging his hands into his front pockets and rocking back and forth on his heels.

"The book? Your book?"

"No, mine," Maya said. "We opened my book from my birth mother and this blackness came out of it and spread on the wall. Merlin, along with Kya and Riebl, appeared as if in a movie. Merlin was bound to a chair." Maya paused, looked up into Adrianna's eyes and continued, "I'm so sorry, Adrianna. Merlin's face was badly beaten."

Teagan watched as Adrianna moved purple streaked hair out of Maya's eyes giving her a small smile. "Tell me what else happened."

"Kya gave us a message," Maya continued. "When she was done the blackness exploded throwing us all backwards. I must have hit and cut my arm when I fell. I think I might have hit the bench."

"I'm going to take Maya back to the house and take care of her arm. The rest of you look around and see if maybe Kya left something behind so we can find them." Adrianna threw her long, white blonde braid back over her shoulder as she put her arm around Maya, pulling her close. "Roam, make sure you get Maya's book and bring it to the house." With the snap of her fingers, she disappeared with Maya.

Teagan watched as Rune kept his gaze from hers and began to search around the tree house. He carefully picked up Maya's book from off the floor, closing it, and handing it off to Roam. For five more minutes, they all searched, but nothing had been left behind. No blackness, no remnants of where Kya and Riebl were keeping Merlin. Nothing.

"Well, that's that," Rove said, pushing one of the benches under the picnic table. "Nothing. How are we going to find them?"

"With the message Kya left for us," Roam answered, kicking another bench towards the picnic table. He leaned forward, placing his hands on the table, looking up at Rove. "I thought we were done with Kya and Riebl," he said, flicking blue streaked hair out of his eyes. "How is it they now have Pappy and not the other way around?"

"Merlin said she had strong powers, stronger than he thought she should have," Vlad answered. "Either she was able to use her powers or someone else let them out."

"But I thought Merlin's castle was made specifically for someone like Kya," Rove said, folding his arms across his chest. "So she wouldn't be able to use her powers and get out."

Vlad raised his arms in defeat. "I don't know, Rove. I'm grasping at straws here. The important thing now is we have to find a way to get Merlin back, and Kya and Riebl locked back up."

"And the way to do that would be for all of us to head to the house," Dimitri stated, putting his arm around Roam's shoulders and steering him toward the ladder. "With all of us here, someone should be able to come up with some kind of solution to get us headed in the right direction."

"Sounds like a plan," Radek said, following his brother and nephew down the ladder.

"You coming, Teagan?"

Teagan looked up to see Diego looking at her with Posh standing behind him. Diego's stance still looked uncomfortable even after a month of being her friend. He had once been on Riebl's side, mainly used as a personal punching bag. Diego had chosen to join with Posh, after discovering she had been an imposter spying on Godard for Vlad. He ran his hand nervously over his newly cropped, black hair drawing his eyes from side to side, a nervous habit he was trying to break.

"In a minute," Teagan answered with a smile as she hung back. She sat on one of the window ledges not really sure if she should follow her friends or not. She felt like an outsider. The only reason she was here was because Vlad had made her. She looked around the now empty space amazed at what the boys had. It was massive. With everyone in here, they had enough room to move and to search, only bumping into each other when someone hadn't been paying attention. She stood, running her hand along the smooth tabletop of the picnic table, suddenly making her long for her home in Ireland with its homemade furniture her dad had made.

"Hey, Teagan!" She jumped slightly, turning around to see Rove, his arms resting on the top rung of the ladder, smiling. She was beginning to see the differences in these brothers, in their mannerisms and facial expressions. But without Rove's look of defiance, she had thought, for just a moment, that Rune had come back for her. "Didn't mean to scare you. You find something?"

Teagan shook her head, giving Rove a small smile. "No, I thought maybe I had, but it was nothing." She ran her fingertips over the tabletop before following Rove down the ladder.

3

MERLIN FELT THE PLAY OF HIS BONDS AS HE TURNED HIS WRISTS AND ANKLES this way and that. He wiggled his torso, but that too was tightly bound to one of his very own kitchen chairs. Shaking his head in disbelief, he looked through swollen eyes around his locked cell in his very own dungeon.

On the highest point of Mount McKinley in Alaska, sits the most magically secured castle of the magical community. Merlin had constructed it himself, made by magic of the highest-ranking wizard still alive, unable to be penetrated by any other magical being. Or at least it had been. What a surprise when Kya and Riebl had suddenly appeared in his kitchen in the castle where he had been holding them. He had just finished making a most delectable tea of jasmine and honey, which now lay splattered all over his newly remodeled kitchen floor, wasted. Kya was a sorceress, of that he was sure. He had thought she was a lower ranking sorceress, but with this latest development, he now questioned his own judgment. The only way for him to figure it out would be to magically scan the castle, but by the time he would be able to do the scan the magical traces Kya had left behind would already be long faded away.

Merlin tried to stomp his foot only to be reminded his ankles were strapped to his chair. "Dang nabbit!" he muttered to himself while closing his eyes and attempting to reach out telepathically, hoping to reach his granddaughter, Adrianna, or one of his grandsons. But each time he tried, he ran into a magically produced barrier constructed by Kya. This woman was irritating him on so many levels! Merlin knew he could penetrate the barrier, he had done it before, but he would need to be touching it to do so. Somehow, Kya had blocked his ability to use his wizard powers to leave his cell.

He muttered an obscenity, thrashing out in his bonds knowing he looked like a toddler having a tantrum. In utter frustration, so unlike himself, Merlin leaned his head back and roared out a yell until his lungs were empty and tears stung his eyes. He let his head fall forward until his chin hit his chest. Whatever his thoughts were telling him, he knew he could not give up or give in. Kya was unstable, of that he was certain. He had to find a way to outwit her and get to his family before he lost everyone he loved. In order to do that he would need to stay calm, to think things through thoroughly and watch for that one flaw, that one mistake, which would allow him to use his powers and escape.

———

RUNE KEPT his eyes trained on the back door while he half listened to the conversations around him. There wouldn't be much talk of what happened in the tree house before Rove returned, so he knew he was safe ignoring the discussion. He just wished Rove would hurry up. What was taking so long? He drummed his fingers on the breakfast bar until the door finally swung open and Rove stepped inside.

"Here she is little bro, safe and sound," Rove said telepathically, as Teagan walked in behind him. *"You're really going to have to figure out how to talk to her, she is only a girl you know."*

Rune nervously ran a hand through his white streaked hair, hearing a snort of laughter next to him. Leave it to Rove to keep his mind open to include Roam in on the conversation. *"Thanks, Rove. Appreciate you making a fool of my discrepancy."* He averted Rove's eyes and watched as Teagan stopped next to Posh and Diego, leaning against the wall next to her friends. He tried, really hard, not to stare at her bellybutton ring.

"He didn't mean anything by his comment, Rune," Roam said inside his head. *"He's only giving..."*

"...me a hard time," Rune finished out loud. "Yeah, I get it. Ha, ha."

His mom looked questioningly at him. "What's going on?" She looked between him and Roam while she placed a bandage on Maya's arm. "Something I should know about?"

"Nope, all's good." Rune smiled, while purposely avoiding looking in Teagan's direction. "Rove's back. How about we get this discussion done? We got some evil beings to hunt."

"If there is something going on between you three..."

"All's good, Mom. Just like Rune said," Rove interrupted, going to the fridge and grabbing out a can of pop.

"I would appreciate if you would refrain from interrupting me," she replied sternly, turning toward Rove.

"Nothing's going on, Mom," Rove answered, tossing a can to Diego then Posh. "Gee, get a grip."

All discussion stopped as Rune watched his mom cross her arms over her chest and stare at her oldest son. First, the refrigerator door slammed shut, making Rove take a step back, then all evidence of the first aid kit vanished from sight. His mom hadn't snapped any fingers, her previously randomly used powers were coming back full force without her need to use anything but her mind to control them.

"Take a seat, Rove. Now," she said, as his can of pop exploded in his hand, sending pop spraying in all directions, and soaking his red T-shirt. "Would you like help in finding a seat?" she asked as Rove's eyes met hers. Without another word, Rove shook off his hands and slowly backed up until he reached a vacant high backed stool next to Rune, and slid onto it.

Mom took a visible, calming breath as she turned her attention to her children and Maya. She absently waved her hand in the direction of the sprayed pop magically erasing all traces. "Which one of you is going to start telling me what's happening here?"

"Did any of you notice your mom didn't snap her fingers?" Rune heard Maya ask as she sat back slightly in her chair to place her injured arm in her lap. Maya wasn't always telepathic. It was a gift given to her from the prophecy so she could converse with them.

"You really did it this time, Rove," Roam said, placing an arm around Maya's shoulders.

"Yup, any suggestions on what I should do about it?" Rove asked, while slightly leaning back on the stool crossing his arms across his very wet chest.

"You could be the one to start talking?" Rune suggested, stealing a look in his mom's direction. She wasn't looking any happier, in fact, she was beginning to look a little scary.

"Done speaking telepathically?" Mom said, her voice rising as she began to tap her bare foot on the floor, her skirt swaying slightly. "Need I remind you I can listen in if I choose to? Would you like me to do that now?"

"Sure, honey. Why don't you do that while someone else tells me what's going on here," Dad said as he walked in from the living room, followed closely by Vlad and Radek. He placed a hand on Mom's shoulder while he glared at his sons.

"I got a little cocky," Rove said, his stool beginning to rock slightly.

"Well, that's no surprise." A smirk appeared on Vlad's face.

"At Mom."

The smirk left Vlad's face. He patted Rove on the shoulder, and moved across the room to lean against the counter by the sink. "I think I'll stay out of this one and let you handle it, Dimitri."

Dad's eyebrows lifted in surprise at Rove. "How's that working out for you?"

"Not too well at the moment."

"This is where an apology would work out well," Roam said telepathically. *"I don't think you want to put your foot in your mouth with Dad as well, do you?"*

A small huff escaped Rove's lips. He lifted his head and looked at their mom. "I'm sorry, Mom. I was out of line."

Mom, still wearing her angry face, fidgeted under Dad's kneading fingers on her bare shoulders. "I accept your apology, Rove. Next time, it would be nice if you could come to the conclusion of an apology *without* anyone else's help." She looked between the four of them, tapping her fingers on one of her crossed arms. "I'm still waiting for an explanation."

Rune opened his mind wide, including his brothers and Maya's, sending out feelers until he found a window open to his mom's thoughts. Giving a gentle push, he waited patiently until his mom opened her mind to him. *"Rove was giving me a hard time about not being able to talk to Teagan,"* he said silently, watching as his mom's eyes met his. *"Maybe we could wait to talk about this until later?"* Rune asked hopefully.

Mom visibly relaxed, her eyes full of sympathy as she nodded. "Others are waiting to hear what Kya and Riebl said, and needing to decide if they should stay. I want the truth, boys. Not some fabricated story so you four can go off, and think you can save Merlin on your own."

"Have you ever heard of a book named, Light and Dark?" Rune quickly asked before his mom changed her mind.

Mom scrunched her eyebrows and shook her head. Rune could almost see her anger vaporize out of her. "No, I don't think so. Why?"

"Because Kya said we needed to bring the Book of Light and Dark with some key, on a day without a night, and she would return Pappy to us."

Mom's face scrunched in thought as she mumbled what he'd said to herself. She looked to Dad who shook his head and shrugged in response, before returning her gaze to her children and Maya. "Kya didn't elaborate anymore on the details? Any indication on which key or where to find this book she wants, or even what she means by 'a day without a night'?"

"The only other thing she said," Maya answered, "was that my book, the one my birth mother left for me, would aid us in finding the key and the location of where we would meet."

"Obviously your book isn't the book she wants," Mom stated absently, turning away from them all and beginning to pace. She rubbed her forehead as if in deep concentration before turning back and raising her eyes to them. "My recommendation would be for us to move into the living room, write down exactly what Kya said, and start looking through Maya's book. I think you boys should bring out your book as well, the one with the prophecy in it. Maybe there will be something in there that can help."

"We'd like to help too, even if it is for us to only read through books."

Rune turned. Maya's parents, Chuck and Jenna Stewart, must have been standing in the doorway to the living room all this time. Rune felt a pang of guilt looking at them. Last time they had been put under a spell from Vlad, so they didn't know their daughter was in any danger, and keeping the Gustavo secret a secret. Maya's parents had learned the truth, only after

Jenna had been kidnapped by the rogue vampires to be used as bait, to bring them all where the battle was to end. Jenna had watched her daughter sacrifice herself to stop immortality for the rogue vampires. Thankfully, Maya's birth mother, the Sorceress of the Sun, had brought Maya back to them all.

Maya got off her stool, went to her parents, and took one of their hands into each of her own. "That's a wonderful idea. We could use all the help we can get."

Conversation started all around as drawers were opened, contents of notebooks and pens removed. Someone tossed a pen in Rune's direction, rolling across the countertop until he stilled it with his fingers. For some reason he looked up in the direction of Teagan. She was still standing in the same spot as before watching as everyone slowly congregated to the spacious living room. Getting off his stool, Rune silently gave himself a push of confidence and took a few steps toward the doorway. He took a calming breath before he turned and looked directly into Teagan's eyes.

"You joining us, Teagan?" he asked, pleased his voice came out confident and strong.

He was somewhat shocked to see surprise alight her face as she pushed away from the wall and simply answered, "Sure."

4

THE HOUSE WAS QUIET, AN UNFAMILIAR HUSH ROLLED LIKE FOG THROUGHOUT the Gustavo home as Teagan made her way up the basement steps and into the kitchen. Someone had left the light on above the kitchen sink giving the room a comfortable glow, and illuminating the clock's face just below the light reading four a.m. Teagan yawned, rolling her stiff shoulders. She raised her arms over her head, leaning back slightly, twisting from side to side. A sigh of relief escaped her lips when she was rewarded with several pops and the immediate loosening of back muscles. She bent at the waist, relaxing her body as her fingertips skimmed the tiled floor. She stood, placing her hands on her hips and turning from side to side while she looked around the kitchen. She loved this house. It always made her feel welcome. The sunny, yellow walls imparting a summer day feel, while the oak cupboards made it look slightly rugged.

Running her fingertips across the cabinet fronts, Teagan made her way to the spacious living room with its hunter green walls and comfortable furniture. She stopped only long enough to grab a bottle of water out of the fridge, thinking she might as well take a look at the progress they had made and see if she could add anything more. Stepping through the doorway, Teagan froze with her fingers mid-turn on the cap of the water bottle.

They had continued to work after she'd gone downstairs. Not two feet in front of where she stood, Rove lay prone on the floor with one arm under his head like a pillow as he slept. His other arm was at his side, the tennis ball he had been tossing earlier just inches away from his fingertips seeming to taunt him. Roam was on the L of the L shaped couch with Maya curled up next to him. Her feet were tucked up underneath her while her head rested on Roam's chest, his chin touching the top of her head. Maya's book lay open across Roam's lap, while the notebook Maya had been writing notes in lay hanging open down the front of the couch.

When Teagan's eyes sought out Rune, her heart skipped a beat when she saw him, almost making her want to bolt from the room. He was sprawled out on his stomach on the other end of the couch. Their large book lay open on the coffee table pulled close with Rune's hand resting on the open pages. His face was totally visible, his white streaked raven hair, for some unknown reason, was pulled away from his face instead of falling over his eyes as it usually did.

He was handsome, no doubt about it, making it difficult for Teagan to pry her eyes away as she watched him sleep. She knew he liked her, his nervousness made that abundantly clear, but Teagan hadn't planned on having a relationship with anyone. Her life was filled with pain and sorrow and she was desperately trying to find her own way, make her own path. She was starting to do that when Vlad had said she had to come to their graduation party, making everything she had felt for Rune from the last time she was here, come creeping back. He made her smile and laugh, her knees to feel weak and her toes to tingle. Her nightmares were non-existent whenever he was around, and she felt herself wanting to be near him whenever he was within eyesight.

"Love will come to you one day. You'll meet many boys, but only one will make your body dance on the inside. And when you look at him, really look, your body will shiver from your toes all the way up your spine to the top of your head. This is when you'll know you've met the one you're destined to be with.'"

It came as a shock to her, her mom's words, they echoed in her mind bringing back the memory of when Teagan was eight-years-old and had asked how she would know she was in love. She hadn't thought of her mom in a long time, making tears spring to her eyes. Her mom, with her blonde hair trailing down her back, or braided in a French braid, with her loving warm brown eyes trained on Teagan. She always had a quick smile, which led to easy laughter, and arms spread wide ready to hug and to hold.

The memory faded, bringing the still sleeping Rune into Teagan's sight. Her chest felt tight as she stared at him until she felt the panic reach the surface, ready to explode. With careful, measured steps, Teagan made her way back into the kitchen and quietly out the back door.

THE BOOK CLUNKED from its weight as Kya set it on the table in between two black pillar candles, with a white candle at the top. With the wave of her hand, and a mere thought of flame, each candle lit at the exact same time casting the only light in the recently cleared small utility room in the dungeon. She smiled as she ran her long black, pointed, fingernails over its charred cover depicting a crudely carved, inverted pentagram. This book would be her salvation. She laughed as she carefully opened its cover, running her fingertips over the slightly blackened pages. How she wished she could see the mighty Merlin's face when he figured out he wouldn't be able to use his powers and escape. The spells this book contained! Soon, very soon, the magical community would bow to her.

"What are you doing in here?"

Kya looked up in time to see the room's only door swing open, causing a draft of stale, musty air to swirl around her. She watched in alarm as the flames from the candles began to sway, her hand frozen on one blackened page. Only when she was sure the flames were going to stay intact, did she look up into the bored face of the most worthless vampire in her employ. "You dolt!" she hissed, careful to keep her own breath away from the candles. "Did it ever occur to you that what I am doing is none of your business?"

Riebl stepped closer to the table, looking down at the opened book. "Another book, Kya? And this one you have to have a candle party with?" He reached down to play with the flame of the white candle.

"If you so much as put out that flame," Kya said, her voice quieter than normal, "we will both be spending the rest of our days in hell."

Riebl froze, slowly pulling his hand away to hang awkwardly at his side. "What exactly are you doing?"

At first, Kya rolled her eyes; she had so much work to do and this idiot was keeping her from it. But, then again, a short lesson probably would be to her favor and keep him away.

"I am looking for spells to use against the wizard and his brats. This book contains...certain spells. Without the candles this book shows spells of questionable use for some, but with the candles, it opens a door, so to speak, of spells of the most vicious magnitude." Kya looked up, pointing at the candles. "The black candles, when lit, open the black magic contained inside this book." She was pleased when she saw Riebl nervously look at her, and take a step back. Good. "The white candle," she continued, "keeps me or anyone else with me, from being pulled into its pages and kept there for all eternity."

Riebl took another step back, grasping tightly with one hand on the hilt of his sword sheathed at his side. "Why would you want to use a book which can take your life, Kya?"

She laughed. "Because it will ensure my defeat of Merlin and his family. Now go away. I have important work to do here. Do not disturb me again when I am in this room. Understand?"

"Yeah, I understand," Riebl answered, walking to the door and very carefully closing it behind him.

Kya smiled, turning her attention back to the book in front of her. Turning its pages carefully until she found the one she wanted. "This will do nicely," she said as she began to read, purposely skipping the warning of the consequences of using a spell of black magic. She didn't care, she wanted power and the more power she obtained, the stronger she would become until no one, not even the highest sorceress, could beat her.

5

THERE WAS NOTHING IN THE WORLD LIKE WATCHING THE SUNRISE FROM somewhere high with nothing obstructing your view. Teagan leaned back on her hands on the roof of an abandoned barn, her legs stretched out in front of her. She closed her eyes, arching her back to feel the heat of the sun on her face and skin. She loved this, the solitude and beauty only the morning sun could give. Sighing, she ran her fingers through her short hair, feeling her head tingle as her hair sprang back to its original place. No matter how hard she tried, she couldn't keep her mind from wandering to thoughts of Rune.

Giving a soft grunt of dissatisfaction, Teagan brought her head up and looked off across the lush green meadow. Grass, weeds and wildflowers had long ago taken over the abandoned fields, making a picturesque scene. It wasn't as green as Ireland's fields, nor as thick, but it still gave her a little pang of longing in her heart for her homeland so far away. She had found this spot just a few weeks ago, after the battle with Godard and his rogue, psychotic vampires. It gave her peace then, but today it brought back the words of a mother she wished she could forget. Words that made her think of Rune.

She sat up, drawing her legs in to crisscross in front of her. She lazily placed her hands in her lap and finally let her feelings and thoughts surface.

What was it that drew her to Rune? It couldn't be his looks; he had two brothers who looked exactly like him, minus the white streaks in his hair of course. Why wasn't she drawn more to Rove? He was more like her—bullheaded, tough, and fearless. A smile escaped her lips as she recalled her first encounter with the brothers. Rove had been standing nose-to-nose with the infamous Dracula. Rove's temper had gotten the best of him, and he had actually flipped the one he should've been most fearful of right onto his back on the ground.

Roam, the middle brother, wasn't her type. He was the practical one. He thought most things through, knowing what needed to be done first. He was calm, gentle, and easygoing. He loved Maya with all his heart and soul, wearing it on his sleeve for all to see. Teagan wondered would she ever love someone that much? And with one look, all would know how much she loved another human being. Was Rune that someone?

Just thinking his name made her heart flutter. He was so funny, so spontaneous, and yet so shy where she was concerned. He often didn't pick up on the seriousness of a situation until it was upon him, but was able to react quickly showing that spontaneity could be a good thing. He seemed to possess traits from each of his brothers; he was both fearless and tactful. But his sense of humor shined through it all. Maybe that was what drew her to him—his ability to make her laugh, even when she didn't want to. It seemed as if her mother's words were right; she had found the one who made her body dance from the inside.

Pressure began to build in her mind and Teagan dropped her head between her knees and closed her eyes tight. She mentally counted to ten before opening her mind, and allowing whoever was trying to contact her through. She groaned loudly as she heard Vlad's voice asking her to come to the cabin.

Without bothering to answer, Teagan stood, placing her hands on her waist to stare out across the fields. She looked all around the barn and on the ground below, making sure no one had wandered into her safe haven before she shot from the roof and into the sky. She loved the feel of the air as her body punched into it, defying gravity as she let loose. She traveled at top speed until the cabin came into sight and she had to slow down to land inside the woods. As she walked the rest of the way to the cabin, she spotted

Vlad and Radek in deep conversation. Teagan was surprised to see Vlad in black cargo shorts, black sandals, and a sleeveless black t-shirt standing in the direct rays of the sun. She snickered as she remembered Rove throwing a bottle of sunscreen at the infamous Dracula to ward off skin cancer.

"I don't see any reason why you and Francesca can't stay at the cabin for as long as you like," Vlad was saying as she quietly walked up behind them. "I will talk to Teagan about it as soon as she gets back."

"Talk to me about what?" Teagan planted her feet on the ground, crossing her arms over her chest as she watched Vlad and Radek spin around.

"Good. This saves time." Vlad smiled at her, taking a step in her direction. She cautiously took a step back, raising her eyebrows in challenge, making him stop.

"It's nothing bad, Teagan," Vlad said, smiling. "In fact, I think you might agree."

"Agree to what?" Teagan moved one of her feet sideways, for a quick get-a-way.

"Francesca and I are going to be staying in the cabin for a while," Radek answered, the cabin door opening behind him and Francesca and Aradney stepping out. "We would like you to come and stay with us."

Teagan took a step backwards. Too many people were looking at her making her nervous. "Why? What did I do?"

"I assure you, Teagan, you've done nothing wrong." Vlad took a cautious step forward. "We thought maybe you'd like to be around kids your own age."

"*You*, all of *you*, thought I'd like to be around kids my own age?" Teagan asked, pointing at them, the sense to flee gnawing at her as she took another step back. "Who died and made you the boss of me?"

The words had come out without her even thinking. She looked from one startled face to the next as the impact of the words slammed into her gut making it hard for her to breathe. Her hand went to her mouth as tears sprang to her eyes, and her feet began to move the minute Vlad and the others made a move towards her. She heard her name shouted as she turned her back on those who cared about her the most, running full tilt into the forest.

Teagan wiped away tears until she took to the sky where the wind dried them for her. She flew until images of her dad overwhelmed her, making her land in some unknown place where the trees were thick and no one would find her. As soon as her feet stumbled to the ground, she fell to her knees burying her face in her hands and cried.

6

RUNE HEARD THE SCREEN DOOR WHINE ON ITS HINGES AS IT WAS THROWN open beyond its capacity, just moments before his Uncle Radek came rushing into the kitchen. He scanned faces before settling on his brother, Dimitri. "Is Teagan here?" he asked apprehensively.

"We haven't seen her since last night," Dad answered.

Radek dragged a hand down his face, turning toward Francesca. "I don't know why I thought she'd come here."

"We'll find her, Radek," Francesca answered, running her hand lovingly down his face to rest on his cheek. "She doesn't have anywhere else to go and we are all she has."

"And unfortunately we've scared her off," Vlad added as the screen door slapped shut behind him. "She didn't return to the cabin. I think she will show up when she is ready."

"If she wasn't so blasted fast we could've caught up with her," Radek answered, pushing through Francesca only to be stopped by Vlad.

"She's been angry before," Vlad reminded him, placing his hand firmly on Radek's chest. "She knows how to get here. She'll come when she's ready."

"But *this* has never happened before," Radek said, pushing against Vlad. "This was a bad idea. I shouldn't have even suggested it."

"Suggested what, Radek?" Dad asked, his chair squeaking slightly as he pushed away from the breakfast table and standing. "Maybe if we knew what's going on we can help you in finding Teagan."

Radek turned around. "As Aradney said, we are all Teagan has. I thought maybe she would like to get to know some kids her own age, to have some fun like a kid. So, I thought maybe I would ask Teagan to stay at the cabin with Francesca and myself so she could be around the boys and Maya."

"She thought she was in some kind of trouble and took off on us," Francesca added.

"I think she was feeling as if I was trying to get rid of her," Vlad said. "That I was leaving her."

"And she already has abandonment issues," Aradney explained.

"Teagan's family left her with you?" Maya asked, surprised.

"No," Vlad answered. "Teagan's mom left her when she was small. Her dad was a friend of a friend of mine, and when they lost their home in Ireland, my friend asked them to come and stay with us. Teagan was ten when they came and joined us. Other than having one friend, she has been mostly around adults for six years. Then last year her dad was killed by one of Godard's followers." Vlad turned, drawing his eyes to look at his grandsons and Maya sitting at the breakfast bar. "We thought getting to know you four would be good for her."

"Not to sound chastising here, but if we would've known that, we could've made a better effort in including her in the things we've done," Rove said, swiveling his stool towards Vlad. "We've tried. We just didn't push the issue." He smiled. "Although, with all the drooling Rune has done over her it's a surprise we haven't scared her off before now."

"Very funny, Rove," Rune muttered.

"This may be even better for her then we thought," Aradney said, exchanging looks with Francesca.

"Where would you like for us to start looking for Teagan, Vlad?" Dad asked, moving toward the door.

"No need," Rune stated. Not only was he able to detect danger, he was also able to sense when others were where they shouldn't be. "She's already here pacing by the tree house. She's pretty agitated."

"Maybe we should go and talk to her," Maya said looking at her friends. "Maybe she won't feel so pressured."

"Actually," Rune said, standing, "I'd like to try and talk with her myself first." He rocked back on his heels. "If that's okay, I mean."

"This ought to be good," Rove said, a smirk on his face. "You can't even say a coherent word when she's around and you want to go out and speak with her alone?"

"At least I'm willing to try," Rune said, turning his back on his brother and walking out.

———

HE WASN'T REALLY sure what he was going to say to her, but if he turned into a blubbering idiot every time she was around, he was never going to be able to win this fight. It's just that every time he looked at her he lost all thought. And her Irish lilt was to die for.

"You better get a grip there, little brother," Rove's voice said in his head. *"And remember, she's just a girl."*

Rune felt his cheeks heat up as he walked toward the tree house. *"Shut up, Rove."* He put up a block so he couldn't hear his brother's jeering anymore, and concentrated on what he should do and say. Teagan wasn't pacing at the bottom of the tree house anymore; she was up inside it. It startled Rune when he realized he could feel her sadness. His gifts were expanding and it scared him a little when thinking of what else he may be able to do. Taking a deep breath, he shoved his worries to the back of his mind, grabbed the ladder, and began to climb.

She was sitting at the picnic table as he poked his head through the door, her back to him. She looked like a little kid with her head in her hands on the table, her shoulders moving as she cried softly. He checked his pocket to make sure the Kleenex Maya had given him were still there and climbed the rest of the way in. He cleared his throat to let her know he was there, but before he could say anything, Teagan seemed to jump and spin at the same time, grabbing his arm and flipping him. He landed on his back on the floor with a thud, the wind knocked out of him.

"Oh, crud," he heard Teagan say as he struggled to take a breath, rolling over on his side as she knelt down next to him. "I'm so sorry. I didn't mean to do that."

"It's okay," Rune finally managed to say. "I get thrown on the floor all the time." He placed a hand onto the floor and pushed up until he was half sitting, looking over at her. Her small frame had just thrown him as if he were a rag doll.

"Here, let me help you up." Teagan extended a hand and gave a small laugh as Rune just stared at it. "I'm not going to flip you again, if that's what you're afraid of, Rune."

He tried not to think how good his name sounded coming from her lips as he took her hand and allowed Teagan to pull him to his feet. He felt as if he towered over her when he stood, at least a foot taller than her, then he made the mistake of looking at her. Even with her face red from crying, Teagan was beautiful. The color of her eyes were this strange transparent brown surrounded by long, thick lashes free of makeup. Her nose was decorated with freckles across its bridge and was as petite as she was, with lips the lightest of pinks. Her round face was encircled by short cropped, copper brown hair, which wisped out in different directions, giving him a sudden urge to run his fingers through it. He could've stood like that forever if only she hadn't broken the spell.

"You okay?"

Rune cleared his throat, taking a step back. "Remind me not to come up behind you again, without your knowledge."

"Sure thing," she answered, stuffing her hands into the front pockets of the same Capris she had on yesterday.

Not knowing if he felt light-headed because of what she did, or because he was in the same room with her, Rune snagged one of the benches and sat down facing her. He placed his forearms on his thighs and leaned forward slightly, giving himself a mental kick and spoke. "Where did you learn to do that?"

"The flipping thing?" Teagan asked. When Rune nodded, she took a shaky breath and looked at her feet. "My dad, a long time ago."

"That's a good thing he taught you."

Rune watched as she seemed to struggle for a moment before a flood of tears trailed down her face. He had to make himself stay sitting while grabbing the Kleenex, shaking one lose and handing it to her.

"I'm sorry," she said, wiping at her eyes. "Once I start, I can't seem to stop." Her emotions seemed to win and she turned away from him.

"Sometimes it helps to talk about things," Rune hurriedly said, trying to keep her from bolting.

There were a few minutes of silence before Teagan answered him quietly, her back still to him. "You ever lose someone you cared about?"

"When I thought Maya died a month ago, I remember how that made me feel," Rune answered, toying with the rest of the Kleenex still in his grasp. "I was angry that someone who fought so hard and saved others from harm was taken away. I thought that I would never find anything to heal my broken heart."

Rune couldn't see Teagan's face, but knew she was still crying when she wiped her face. "My mom left us, my dad and me, when I was eight." Teagan began slowly, her lilt more evident from her emotions as she began turning around. "My dad was a daywalker like you, my mom a mortal. When I was born I took on the traits of my dad, and I don't think my mom could handle that." Without looking at Rune, Teagan sat down on the bench adjacent to his with her body facing the door. She accepted the Kleenex from Rune, offering a small smile of thanks as she wiped her face again.

"My dad took real good care of me. He taught me how to ride a horse, milk cows, and chop wood with an axe. When I got older, I hadn't grown too much so my dad taught me how to defend myself. And when we lost the farm and had nowhere to go, his nightwalker friend introduced us to Dracula. Vlad took us in, gave us a home and my dad a job."

"Vlad told us your dad died last year," Rune said quietly. "I'm sorry."

Teagan nodded, more tears falling. "Yeah. He had run into a group of Godard's followers. There was a fight. My dad lost."

Rune reached over without thinking and touched her arm.

"He died in my arms."

Rune didn't care what she thought. He stood abruptly from the bench, pulling Teagan to her feet. He took a moment to look into her startled, tear filled eyes before pulling her into his arms, giving her no choice but to accept his empathy. When he thought she was trying to pull away, he held her tighter, and when her body began to shake, he placed his cheek on the top of her head and comforted her as she cried.

7

─────────

With anger flaring, Kya stepped around the rectangular table facing the contents sitting on its wood surface. With one arm, she cleared the tabletop, glass shattering, spewing splinters everywhere. She turned with hands raised, her long black fingernails gleaming in the artificial light to glare at the man she held captive. He was giving her a pounding headache.

"You know," Merlin said from the chair he was still strapped to, "that was a perfectly good crystal ball." He shook his head. "What a shame."

"Shut up!" Kya yelled watching spittle fly as her temper flared. "Do you have a death wish?" She stomped around the castle's kitchen, her arms flailing as she stared at the oldest wizard still on earth. "All I want is a book and a miserable key, is that too much to ask!"

Merlin smirked. "You know as well as I do that you can't kill me, Kya. You're strong, but not that strong."

Whirling around, she imagined making a scissors appear and chopping off the long white beard of the infamous Merlin. She let a smile play across her lips, as she looked her prisoner in the eye. "I can do more than you think, old man," Kya said as she took a deep breath and attempted to pull herself together. "Now, once again, where is the gateway to the Enchanted Realm?"

Merlin tsked, "Do you really think I would be that stupid, Kya?"

Kya smiled eerily, running one long fingernail across the bridge of his bruised nose. "I would think you would want to keep your grandsons and family from harm." She snapped her fingers making her pawn appear. She was pleased with this new handy spell she had found in one of her spell books. The snap was just for show, of course. Riebl appeared in front of her, a polishing rag in one hand, and his trusted sword in the other.

"Really, Kya?" the nightwalker said perturbed, giving his sword one last swipe with the rag before placing the sword in its sheath at his side. "You couldn't just call me?"

Kya allowed a growl to escape her lips and watched as Riebl took a step backward. "I need you to go to the Gustavo house and cause a little scene," she said, through gritted teeth. "Do you think you can do that?"

Riebl smiled. "What did you have in mind?"

"Bring me Adrianna Gustavo's hair."

"Are you insane?" Riebl said incredulously, placing a hand on the hilt of his sword. "I won't be able to get anywhere near her for she wields Excalibur! She nearly destroyed my sword last time!"

Kya rubbed her forehead. She was beginning to think she'd made a mistake in letting this nightwalker be in her service. "Bring me one of the brothers' necklaces. Can you do that or is that too much to ask?"

"Nah, I can do that," Riebl answered, withdrawing his sword and making it dance in the air. "It'll be fun to meet up with the blue haired freak. Maybe I can knick his neck artery this time." He turned his head and smiled at Merlin. "Since his grand-pappy won't be able to get to him in time."

"Take these," Kya said, interrupting Riebl's laughter and handing him four small bottles, two with orange liquid, one with green, and the last with a swirling black. "Break the black first. It will cover the area with blackness so the sun cannot harm you. The orange bottles will explode if you should need a distraction, and the green will return you to me once you have the necklace."

Riebl stuffed the green and orange bottles into one of his front pockets, keeping the black in his left hand. He stood before her, his sword hanging loosely from his right hand. "Well?" he said.

Kya looked at him, confused.

"Unless you'd like me to take other transportation, it will take weeks before you get your diversion."

Kya absently waved her arm, smiling when Riebl disappeared from sight. She turned her attention once more to Merlin. "It would really be in your best interest to do what I ask."

"And I grow tired of your little tantrums," Merlin said just moments before he vanished from sight.

Kya leaned back, placing her hip on the corner of the tabletop while mentally counting backward from ten. When nothing happened, she calmly waited to the count of five, relaxing when lights began to shimmer in front of her eyes making her smile. When Merlin magically reappeared, still bound to his chair with a look of total disbelief on his face, Kya burst out laughing.

"How?" Merlin stammered. "How did you do this?"

Kya got into the face of the mighty Merlin. "Black magic," she whispered, and laughed into the terrified face of the greatest wizard of all time.

———

DIMITRI STOOD near the back door of his home, hands in the front pockets of his gray cargo shorts, watching his beautiful wife as she stood in the center of the deck. Her hair had been let loose of its binder to trail down her soft, yellow T-shirt, her feet bare. Her head was slightly tilted back as if she were studying the tops of the trees.

She had been standing there for a good half an hour now.

"I'm okay," Adrianna said with her back still to him. "I'm only thinking, and worrying a little."

Dimitri went to her, wrapping his arms around her while her head dropped back onto his chest. "Radek and Vlad went back to the cabin with Francesca and Aradney, to finish moving things in. I've ordered everyone else to wrap things up for a while and get some fresh air."

"That sounds like a good idea," Adrianna answered as a yawn escaped her lips. "Maybe one of us should go and collect the two still in the tree house?"

"I'll send Rove in a few minutes," Dimitri said, smiling when Adrianna chuckled. He snuggled in closer to rest his cheek on hers.

Adrianna placed a hand on the side of his face, rubbing her cheek with his. "I don't know how much time we have to find this key," she said.

"We'll find it in plenty of time to save Merlin," Dimitri answered, kissing her neck.

"But we can't let Kya get what she wants, Dimitri. No good will come of it, we have to stop her at all costs."

"Don't be cryptic, Adrianna," Dimitri answered angrily. "I won't risk losing anyone."

"Then you need to get to Roam immediately," someone said from behind them. "Riebl is coming."

Dimitri spun, pushing Adrianna behind him. "Merlin?" he said, staring in disbelief.

Merlin was strapped to a kitchen chair his lips moving, but no more sound reached Dimitri. Adrianna stepped forward, her hand outstretched in front of her as a haze covered Merlin until he was gone from sight.

Dimitri turned when movement caught his attention. He watched as blackness swirled around the tree house and crawled on the ground towards the deck. Keeping Adrianna behind him, Dimitri brought out his fangs as one of the sides of the tree house blew off, landing almost at his feet.

8

"So, let me see if I have all of this straight." Rune smiled as Teagan tapped her chin with her finger as they sat at the picnic table in the tree house; he thought she looked and sounded adorable. "You and Rove were both born with the streaks in your raven hair, but Roam's blue streaks and Maya's purple streaks were given to them by the prophecy. Maya also received the ability to create a purple barrier which cannot be broken."

"Right," Rune answered as his skin began to tingle. He absently rubbed his arms as Teagan stretched hers over her head.

"Maybe it's because I'm Irish that I believe in magic. But I have to admit I have never seen magic as powerful as all of you."

"We didn't get our powers until the prophecy," Rune answered absently, as the air suddenly changed in the tree house. It was almost like an electric charge, something only Rune could feel. He slowly stood from the picnic table where he and Teagan had been talking, his fangs dropping down as he went to stand in front of her, blocking her from the threat he was feeling.

"What is it?" Teagan asked as she stood, her body tensing, her fangs descending.

"Stay back," Rune responded, his eyes scanning the interior, his senses fully open. His body was humming, tingling, like a massive feeling of skin crawling. It would probably drive anyone else crazy, but for Rune it was normal. He had this uncanny ability to sense danger, just like his brother Roam was able to give others a mind zap. Since the prophecy, his ability advanced into telling him when someone was where they shouldn't be, how many there were, what kind of weapons they had, and where the weapons were on their person.

Rune suddenly spun, grabbing Teagan with his right hand and shoving her back behind him as a ball of white stars materialized in his left hand, with a five dimensional star in the center of it. When the tingling in his body became more insistent and his body began to feel compressed, he made the orb grow larger. When he finally zeroed in on the threat, he turned just as Riebl appeared in the doorway. Rune threw the orb and took out the entire wall where Riebl should have been.

"Where is he?" Teagan shouted from next to him, her head darting from side to side.

Rune held up a hand, his senses on full alert. He slowly took a step toward the doorway, another orb appearing in his hand. He was here. He could feel him. There were several snaps to the air, making Teagan jump back, as Dad with Mom suddenly appeared. Rune took Teagan's hand, pulling her close as more shouting could be heard outside. Dad's fangs were fully descended as well, the color of his eyes red as he looked to Rune.

"Where is he?" he asked.

"He's still here. I can feel him," Rune answered, not even questioning how his dad knew who it was.

"Follow it," Dad commanded, his voice dropping an octave in anger. "He's here for Roam."

Rune's eyes shot to his dad, who nodded in confirmation. Rune pulled Teagan next to his side and shot out of the opening through which his family members had just entered. He landed next to his brothers and Maya, between the house and the tree house, an orb already formed in his free hand. Rove stood tall with a dragon scaled rope in each hand, one set to flame and swishing silently back and forth as if it were alive. Roam's fingers were sparking, blue lightning dancing across his fingertips while Maya held her hands at the ready.

"Is it Riebl?" Rune heard Rove ask silently, but before he could answer his body began to hum.

"Maya! Barrier!"

Maya's barrier popped into existence. Out of instinct, Rune grabbed Teagan, using his own body as a shield until he knew for sure the barrier had gone up in time.

TEAGAN HAD FOUGHT with them just a month prior, but had never actually stood with them shoulder to shoulder. The vibes they were sending out were outstanding, making the adrenaline pump through her veins. It was almost as if the brothers and Maya were all connected and were all feeding off each other. When something exploded off Maya's barrier, she was suddenly in Rune's arms, his back to where the explosion came from. When he turned her back around a purple transparent barrier stood before them.

"You can't break her barrier, you dolt!"

Teagan looked through the barrier. Kya stood behind Riebl, her red hair floating as if a fan were blowing in her face, her long emerald gown billowing around her bare feet. Riebl turned toward Kya, his sword held in front of him.

"You sent me here, Kya. This is my fight!" Riebl yelled, his long black hair whipping in his face. "Go away!"

Teagan felt Rune go rigid just before he let go, but continued to stand next to her, an orb appearing in each hand. Her skin began to crawl, as the energy the brothers and Maya were sending out seemed to engulf her. If she hadn't known the individual colors of the brothers, there would've been no way for her to tell them apart as they stood shoulder to shoulder next to her. As she looked at each of them, she could see their color as a haze around their bodies.

Suddenly, the barrier dropped. Rune threw one of his orbs, and it exploded in front of Riebl sending the nightwalker flying backwards, his sword slipping from his hand. Rove broke from the group, moving to the other side of Teagan, the flame coming off his rope was now extending up his arm and his black T-shirt making it look as if it were on fire. He winked at her just before he brought his second rope to flame. It jumped on the ground as if it were alive wanting to break free.

There were no words coming from the boys and Maya, but each of them seemed to move as if it were choreographed, making Teagan realize they had to be speaking telepathically. She had listened to Vlad during and after the first battle and learned that Maya had earned telepathy from her part in the prophecy. Teagan really wished she knew what was being said. More than ever, she wanted to be a part of this group.

The air suddenly charged, compressing against Teagan's body, like a hug gone too tight and held too long. As she struggled to take a breath, blue lightning zapped the air, hitting the ground in front of Riebl's prone body and making Kya step back. Rove's rope snapped the air behind her, Teagan turned in time to see the rope extending outward and wrap around Riebl's sword, like a snake. Rove pulled back, and dropped the sword at her feet. A hum traveled up her body, starting at her feet. A bright, silvery haze surrounded the sword as she looked down, the sword beginning to fade in and out, as her head began to swim. Teagan turned to look into Rune's questioning eyes just seconds before her legs gave out and she felt herself fall.

"TEAGAN!" Rune yelled, placing his body in front of her still one. He felt Maya's barrier go up and over Teagan as he stared at Riebl across the lawn.

The nightwalker slowly got to his feet, staring back with pure hatred, his eyes flicking to the sword at Rune's feet. When Riebl took a step toward him, Rune made another orb appear, tossing it in his hand as his brothers and Maya came to stand next to him. He cocked his arm back and was disappointed when Kya grabbed Riebl's arm and they vanished from sight. He squished the orb in his grasp, turning to kneel down by Teagan. Maya's barrier dropped when he reached out to touch her, running the back of his hand down her cheek and saying her name softly. He carefully checked her over, looking for any signs of injury.

"I don't think she's hurt, Rune," Roam said, kneeling down next to him. "I think she may have fainted."

Rune carefully scooped Teagan up into his arms, noticing she barely weighed anything at all. He found himself looking to the ground where she had been laying, to check for any signs of blood, until he felt a hand on his arm and looked at his mom now standing next to him.

"Let's get her into the house, Rune, before they decide to come back. I'll look her over and make sure she's okay."

Rune looked down at Teagan, holding her close to his body while carrying her protectively into the house.

9

DARKNESS CONTINUED TO SWIRL AROUND RIEBL'S BODY, GRASPING ONTO HIS black jeans, as Kya let go of him in the middle of the massive kitchen of Merlin's castle. Riebl planted his feet, steadying himself as his anger burned, threatening to combust. The center island was mere inches from him, but no way would he show weakness by grabbing onto one of its corners. He was still getting used to Kya transporting him magically, and hated how it made him feel weak and helpless. He glared at Kya as she threw open a cupboard door, extracting spell books of varying sizes she had replaced the dishes with.

"Why didn't you grab it?" Riebl asked through clenched teeth, as Kya's movements broke apart the last of the blackness to disappear like fog under her hideous dress. When she didn't answer, he grabbed her by the arm and swung her around. "Conjure it! Bring my sword back!"

"I can't," Kya snapped, yanking her arm from his grasp and grabbing yet another book.

"Why not?" Riebl yelled his anger snapping as he grabbed the book from her hands and threw it across the room. He knew immediately that he shouldn't have done that. Kya turned, and he was flying backwards across the room before her arm was fully extended in front of her. He crashed into the pantry doors, its parts raining down on him in chunks and dust. Taking a shaky breath, Riebl looked up into Kya's furious face.

"You are an idiot!" she said, her face red with anger inches from his. "The sword is no longer available for your use! It belongs to her!"

Riebl's mouth was suddenly very dry. "What do you mean it belongs to her?"

Kya stood, backing away from him and shaking her head. She extended her hand behind her back, and the book Riebl had thrown flew into her open hand. "The sword is magically connected to that girl, weren't you paying attention back there?" she said, using the book as a pointer. "How exactly did you obtain the sword?"

Riebl picked himself up from off the floor. "I found it."

"Where?"

Riebl shrugged his shoulders. "I was with Godard probably a year ago. We came across some vampires—one of them had the sword. We fought, the guy dropped the sword and I stabbed him with it. Since mine was long gone, I took it as my own."

"The girl, she wasn't there when you took the sword?"

"No," Riebl answered, brushing debris off his clothing and shaking his head to release the dust in his hair.

Kya began to pace, ignoring the dust and particles showering her. "The sword lit up when it was near her. It is meant for the girl...but I don't think she knows, not yet...you must have killed the one who held it before she was to have it."

Riebl scratched his head, he was never sure if he should speak when she muttered to herself. "If the girl doesn't know it's hers, then why can't you just take it from her?"

"Because the sword knows, you idiot," she answered absently. Kya stopped, her head suddenly snapping up, training her eyes on him as Riebl swallowed nervously. "Did she notice?" Kya asked, stepping towards him. He instinctively took a step back only to be stopped by the broken door behind him.

"Did she notice what?"

Kya huffed out a breath. "Did the girl notice the sword glowed at her feet?"

"No, I don't think so," Riebl answered nervously. "She was watching them."

A smile lit Kya's face. "We have to go back."

"No!" Riebl drew his arm away from Kya's outstretched hand. "Are you crazy?"

"Don't you see? It's our chance." Kya stepped forward to be mere inches from him. "With the sword she gives them more power, without it..."

"...we have a better chance of beating them," Riebl finished uncertainly.

"Exactly." Kya placed her hand on his forearm, and with a laugh, they disappeared.

MUMBLING WAS the first thing Teagan heard as she woke, turning into words being spoken by more than one person. She began to wonder why there were people in her room, and for some reason, was more concerned if she was dressed properly than who the people were. She slowly began to open her eyes to see Rune's staring straight into hers.

"Hey," he said, smiling. "It's about time you joined us."

He sure is cute. Teagan squashed the thought as she stared back at him, giving him a nervous smile. She placed her hands on the sofa cushions and began to push herself up.

"Whoa," Rune said, placing a hand firmly on her shoulder. "You kinda hit your head when you fainted so you're gonna want to take it slow at first. Mom won't like it if you hurl all over the couch."

"I did not faint," Teagan responded, knocking his hand aside and giving Rune a questioning look. "I've never fainted in my life."

Rune placed his hand right back on her shoulder. "Trust me on this," he said, increasing the pressure on her shoulder and giving her a look that would've made his mom proud. "You move too fast too soon and you're not going to feel too great." He pushed more on her shoulder. "Please wait for a little while and I'll help you."

"Can I hurl on you when you help me up?" Teagan smiled sweetly, batting her eyelashes as Rune sat back onto the coffee table. "It's not my fault if I supposedly fainted anyway. All that power made me light headed, and all your colors intermixing made me dizzy."

"Maybe she hit her head harder than you think, Rune," Rove said from one of the wingback chairs behind him.

"What do you mean, Teagan, about our powers and colors?" Roam asked.

Teagan shifted on the couch until Rune grabbed some pillows and placed them behind her, "Thanks," she said giving Rune a smile, then looking back at Roam. She thought it was cute; Roam and Maya snuggled together on the other wingback chair. Roam's dark hair to Maya's light. Something nagged at the back of her mind, something important.

"Teagan?"

She slowly brought her eyes back to Rune's. "What?"

Concern showed in Rune's eyes. "You were going to tell us about our colors surrounding us."

"Maybe she hit her head harder than we thought," Rove repeated, standing. "Mom should probably take a look at her now that she's awake."

Teagan placed her hand on Rune's arm. "I'm okay, really I am. I'm just not sure you'll believe me."

"Why don't you start with our colors?" Maya prompted. "What did you mean about them intermixing?"

Light and dark ran across Teagan's thoughts as Rove returned to sit back in the chair he had vacated. She pushed the thought back in her mind hoping she'd remember and think about it later. "It's the second time I've seen it, the first was when you were all in the tree house earlier. I saw your colors through the window."

"Our colors?" Roam asked, his facial expression questioning. "What do you mean?"

Teagan grasped onto Rune's hand, pulling herself up to sit on the couch. She was grateful when Rune moved from the coffee table to sit next to her, her hand still securely in his. She looked into Rune's eyes. He gave her hand a squeeze and she decided she liked how it felt, finally deciding to relax and see where this took her.

"When all four of you brought out your powers, the air changed," Teagan began, looking between them all. "It was almost like when you step out of an air conditioned house into extreme humidity." She stopped as everyone stared at her. "So, no one has ever told you that?"

"No," Rune said. "Tell us the color part, Teagan."

"Well..." She thought about it for a moment before answering. "It was after you brought out your powers all at the same time. A haze of color surrounded each of you." She looked around as each of them stared at her, fighting the urge to roll her eyes. "The colors surrounding each of you, was the color you have in your hair. If I wouldn't have known the individual colors of you three, I wouldn't have been able to tell you apart. You looked exactly alike."

"But we already look exactly alike," Rune said, giving her a concerned look.

"I know," Teagan said, starting to feel agitated. "But I can tell you and your brothers apart, even if I didn't know your colors. You each behave differently. When you all brought out your powers at the same time it was as if you were all one person."

"Okay, so you are saying that each one of us had our color surrounding us at the same time our powers were out," Maya asked.

Teagan nodded. "Yes, and they intermixed swirling around all of you."

"You really clobbered your head when you fainted," Rove said.

"Quit saying that," Teagan interjected. "This was all before I supposedly fainted."

"It wasn't supposedly," Rune stated. "You looked at me, your eyes rolled to the back of your skull and you hit the ground." He smiled. "It's not that we don't believe you. A lot has happened recently. Things that we thought weren't even possible. We are just trying to understand how you were able to see our colors."

"So, you've seen them before," Teagan stated, crossing her arms over her chest.

"Once," Maya answered. "We all saw our colors, like you described when the boys found me and discovered I was the fourth they were meant to find. When we received our powers from the prophecy, our colors came from each of us, combined, and literally slammed back into all of us at the same time. I haven't noticed our colors since."

"It is possible," Adrianna said as she walked through the doorway from

49

the kitchen, a steaming mug in her hands, "that Teagan is receiving powers just as you four did." She sat on the coffee table across from Teagan, placing the warm mug into her hand.

"But I don't have powers," Teagan said, looking up from the steaming mug into Adrianna's eyes. "Why would I get powers?"

Adrianna shrugged her shoulders with a gleam in her eyes. "Probably because you are surrounded by magical beings. Somewhere in your lineage was probably a witch. Your powers have been dormant until now. And being in the home of a witch and a sorceress, your body can no longer suppress the magic it holds."

"Who's the sorceress?" Maya questioned, sitting more upright in Roam's lap.

"Well, according to Merlin, it is you." Adrianna turned to look at Maya. "Your birth mother is the Sorceress of the Sun. You have powers of your own. You are a sorceress."

Teagan felt Rune stiffen next to her just as she felt something heavy and unseen envelope her body. The only thing she could move were her eyes, as she felt another wave, and Kya and Riebl suddenly appeared in the room.

"Find it!" Kya said, her arms upraised, her hands fully opened and extended.

Riebl smiled, waving his hand in front of Rove's face and laughing when Rove couldn't move.

"Stop messing around, you idiot!" Kya hissed, her hands beginning to shake. "We're on a time limit here. Find it now!"

Riebl turned, scanning the room and stopping when he saw Teagan. He quickly came to her, looking around her, under the coffee table and on the couch. "It's not here!" he said, sounding panicked.

"It's here! Look in the kitchen."

"Is this what you're looking for?" Dimitri appeared in the doorway, Vlad and Radek flanking him with Posh and Diego behind him. Dimiri held up the sword and Teagan watched as the sword wavered until it flew out of his hand and straight into hers, whatever had been attached to her fell away. Teagan stood, her body feeling strange as she looked to the sword in her hand. A silvery haze surrounded it, creeping up her arm until it covered her entire body. She two fisted the sword and found herself feeling the weight of it, familiarity seeping into her mind. She knew this sword was perfectly balanced, and what was etched onto its hilt. She also knew who was the last to hold it, before Riebl had claimed it as his own.

She drew her gaze up and locked eyes with Riebl. The nightwalker was staring directly at her, his face getting redder as his anger flared. Teagan raised the sword, knowledge seeping into her as memories flooded her mind and her heart. She held the hilt of the sword just above her stomach, the double-edged blade turned away from her body as she returned his stare. She moved the tip of the sword to point directly at Riebl, challenging him to come and take it away. She watched as the nightwalker's eyes grew wide as she pulled, splitting the sword into two. A smile lit her face as she knowingly moved her body, bringing her right arm above her head, blade out, and her left in front of her body. She waved her fingers of her left hand at Riebl, taunting him to make a move as a warmth traveled across her left wrist, her dominant arm.

"That's my sword!" Riebl yelled.

"In your dreams," Teagan responded, as Kya grabbed his arm and they once again vanished from sight.

10

ADRENALINE COURSED THROUGH HER VEINS AS TEAGAN KNOWINGLY HELD THE swords, scanning the room for Riebl and Kya. She was going to take them out if it was the last thing she ever did. When she felt a soft touch on her shoulder, she spun and looked into the surprised eyes of Rune.

"Everyone stop!"

At Adrianna's yell, Teagan cautiously looked around. Rove had two flaming ropes out, one arm cocked back. Teagan thought it strange that if he were to let go, his flaming rope would come right at her. She quickly looked behind her to find the threat, but instead there was Roam looking directly at her, blue lightning sparking from his hands extending upward to almost reach the ceiling. What was going on?

"Everyone take a deep breath and stand down," Teagan heard Adrianna say, but she couldn't see her. What exactly did she mean?

"Teagan honey, they're gone. Carefully bring your swords down." Adrianna came into view, a very large sword in her right hand, its tip pointing to the floor. "Everything's alright now, bring your swords down very slowly."

"What?" Teagan answered, her mind felt fuzzy as she slowly looked around the room. Rove still held flaming ropes in his grasp, and Roam was still sending out smaller sparks of lightning. Where was Rune? "You want me to do what?"

"Sword...Teagan." She heard someone say who sounded quite a bit like Rune. "Please...lower your...sword."

Slowly, with fear building, Teagan turned. Her eyes grew wide when she saw Rune pushed up against the wall, a sword at his neck. Her sword. "Oh my god!" Teagan gasped. "What do I do?"

"Relax, Teagan." Vlad was there, right next to her. Sweat began to form on her forehead as she felt Vlad's hand rest carefully on hers. "It's okay," he said, coming into view and smiling at her. "Just relax your arm. I'll help you with your sword."

Her sword, the one Riebl had held was her sword. The same sword her father had once held and protected. Tears welled in her eyes as Vlad carefully brought her left arm down, and pulled Rune out of the way. Tears spilled over as a small trickle of blood traveled down Rune's neck. A sob escaped her lips as Teagan looked at the two swords in her grasp. She slowly began to back up making sure the tips were pointed at the floor.

"Teagan, I'm okay," Rune said, slowly reaching for her.

"No," Teagan cried. "You're not. I'm so sorry. I didn't think I could hurt someone I loved. I'm so sorry." She turned and blindly ran out the door without looking back.

———

"Teagan!" Rune stopped, the tips of his black Converse All Stars dangling over the edge of the back deck. He listened, reaching out with his powers to zero in on which way she had gone. He pushed off from the deck into the sky, pushing his senses out until he felt her and changed his course. He pushed, trying to get into her thoughts to communicate with her, but she was locked up tight. Then, there she was. Walking at a clipped pace through the forest, her swords still split into two.

"Teagan!" Rune called out as his shoes touched the ground two yards behind her. "Teagan!" he yelled again, quickening his pace until he was right behind her. Not worrying about the swords still in her grasp, Rune grabbed her arm and spun her around. "You can't just say something like that and walk out!"

"I think I just did," she snapped back, wiping tears from her cheek and spinning back around.

"Wait, Teagan. Please," he pleaded waiting for her to stop and fisting his hands at his sides. She stalked away, the sunlight filtering through the trees shone on the bling on her Capris making him close his eyes to try to stay on the matter at hand, and pray for patience. "Don't make me stop you!" he shouted. He felt a wave move through his body, making him feel as if he were on a roller coaster until something solid slammed into him. He opened his eyes to find Teagan staring at him, his head feeling a little too light.

"Whoa," he said, grabbing onto Teagan's shoulders to right himself.

"How...?" she stammered. "How did you do that?" She placed her hands on her hips. "Another power you received from the prophecy you didn't bother telling me about?"

Rune took a breath, held up one finger, and then took another. "Don't...know."

She tilted her head as concern lit her face. "Rune, sit down before you fall down."

"Good idea." He plopped down onto the ground, dropping his head into his hands.

Teagan crouched down next to him, the swords tips sticking into the dry earth. "You've never done that before?"

Rune shook his head.

"What exactly did you do?"

Rune ran his hands through his hair and slowly lifted his head. He no longer felt as if the ground was tipping or his lungs compressed. He took a shaky breath and looked at her. She was still crouched down next to him with her swords sticking into the ground.

"I wanted to stop you, and then I did."

"Neat trick."

He looked toward her swords and jutted his chin towards them. "Do you think maybe you could put those away?" he asked.

Teagan huffed out a breath. "I don't know how."

"Can't you just push them back together and send them back to wherever they came from?"

"You don't think I've tried?" Teagan answered sarcastically, plopping down across from him.

Rune dropped his hands, turning his head to the side. "Look, I'm fine. Only a small scratch. It'll be gone soon." When she looked away, Rune reached out and grabbed her chin forcing her to look at him. "Mom wanted me to tell you the same thing happened to her when she first became the protector of Excalibur. Something about an overwhelming desire to fight taking over her senses." He reached over and wiped a stray tear from her cheek.

"You're just saying that to make me feel better," Teagan said, sniffling.

"No, honestly," Rune answered. "Am I right? How it made you feel? How else would I have known if Mom hadn't told me?"

Teagan began to draw lines in the dirt with one of her swords. "I felt..."

"You felt what?" he encouraged.

The lines in the dirt became swirls. "I felt powerful. I felt the knowledge of the sword seep into my mind, into my memories, into my heart. I remembered my dad dying in my arms when Vlad brought him back to the house and I got angry." She swiped away tears and looked at Rune. "All I wanted to do was kill Riebl and Kya."

Rune nodded, "The same thing happened to Roam when Riebl pulled a knife on him. Roam took the knife and held it at Riebl's throat until blood began to trickle down. It took everything Rove and I had to get him to calm down and back off."

"Really?"

"Yeah, really."

Teagan began drawing in the dirt again, intertwining the circles she had already drawn. "Why did you run after me?" she suddenly asked.

"Because you said you loved me." Rune reached out and stilled her hand. "If you really love me, Teagan, you're going to have to start trusting me. I'd never lie to you."

She looked at the two swords, lifting them out of the dirt. "What do you think I should do?"

"Do?"

"What do I do with these? I can't put them back together." She demonstrated by banging them together. "I can't exactly walk around carrying these everywhere I go."

Rune scrunched his eyebrows together and grabbed her left wrist, twisting it to look at the inside of her wrist. "When did you get a tattoo?"

"When the sword first chose me," she answered looking at it. "My grandfather had one just like it." She brought her eyes up and looked at him again. "I still don't know what to do with these."

Rune smiled, letting go of her wrist to cup her chin. "Try taking a deep breath, close your eyes, and visualize the swords going back together."

She rolled her eyes at him. "Really? That's all you've got?"

Rune snickered, increasing the pressure on her chin before letting go. "Just try it, for me."

Teagan huffed out a breath before taking a deep one. She closed her eyes and when she opened them, she brought the swords up. The late afternoon sun gleamed off the swords as if they knew something was going to happen. Teagan bit down on her lip while placing the swords together. Her eyes widened in amazement as the swords magically forged together to form only one.

"Huh," Rune said. "I only did what we told Roam to do when trying to find Maya telepathically. I didn't think it would really work."

"Yeah, you're a dynamo," Teagan answered sarcastically. "But I still have a sword that I can't carry around. Any more ideas?"

"We'll go ask my mom," Rune said chuckling, getting to his feet. He reached out a hand and pulled her up. "Somehow my mom makes Excalibur go away." He turned her wrist over again. "I really want to ask you what this tattoo means, but you'll end up having to retell it when we get home." He weaved his fingers with hers and grasped on tight. "How about it? Ready to head back?"

Teagan smiled. "Sure, on one condition that we stop at the cabin first. I need a change of clothes."

"Deal. Now I can tell everyone we're on our way. They're giving me a headache."

Teagan frowned slightly. "Do you think we'll be able to communicate telepathically?"

"I don't see why not."

"I've tried, but I can't seem to get through."

"Same here," Rune responded. He looked into her eyes and pushed with his thoughts, but no door was open. "You're locked up tight. You have to open up and let me in."

Teagan scrunched her eyes. "How can that be? I always forget to close the door when I'm with Vlad and the others."

"Don't worry about it," Rune answered, running a hand down her cheek. "We'll work on it. You don't think Vlad put up a block on you do you?"

"If he did, I may have to use him for sword practice." With a gleam in her eye and a spring in her step, Teagan pulled on Rune's hand as she began to walk.

"Now that's something I just gotta see," he responded pulling Teagan back to walk next to him side-by-side.

11

Iron bars surrounded him in his own cold, dank dungeon. Merlin sat on the thin mattress on the lone cement slab jutting out from the wall, which served as a bed. His head hung, his fingers toying with the tattered remnants of his wizard robe. He stared at the black strings woven around his wrists, knowing they were preventing him from using his magic and getting free. Kya had strengthened her power in these and replaced them for the ones he had on before. There was no need to try to remove them, they were held fast. There was no need to pace, no magic spells to recite. He had been defeated by black magic. All he could do was sit and wait.

As long as Riebl didn't appear to gloat, he knew Roam and all he cared for were safe. Merlin thought he had crossed all his t's and dotted all his i's in keeping Kya's sorcery contained. He had known she was evil. He never thought she would go as far as she had to try and obtain passage to the most magical place in all the worlds. He brought his eyes up and looked around his nine-by-nine-foot cell. There were no windows to feel the sunlight. There were no other prisoners in the three other cells for him to confide in. Just dull gray cement walls and floors, and one lone light bulb outside the cells. Although he would die before giving Kya what she wanted, he couldn't help but feel he had failed. He felt totally and utterly defeated.

HE HATED THIS PLACE, this castle with its balconies and it's way too many tapestries hanging on its stone walls. There were hundreds of rooms with fancy furniture no one uses, and way too many hallways. Riebl marched up the stone steps to the second level as his temper bordered on rage, the empty scabbard at his side rubbing against his leg. He had no idea why anyone would want to live here in this place of light. Lucky for him that Kya's barrier had made it dark or he would've burned up the moment of his arrival. Doors lined the left side of the hallway, while windows wider than his arm span, and three-fourths of his height, lined the right. Between each door and window were those unremarkable paintings of people he didn't care about. He had lost his sword to a measly girl! The Gustavos were going to pay.

Riebl stopped, taking in jagged breaths, turning to the left to stare at a painting on the wall. The hand-made oak frame meant nothing to him. The fact that the portrait was hand-painted with the richest of oils held no meaning. He reached for his scabbard at his side to find it empty. With flaring temper, Riebl reached to the small of his back and extracted his knife from its sheath, driving it straight through Merlin's face. The sound of the ripping canvas and crackling paint only encouraged him on. He plunged his knife over and over until the painted wizard was a shredded mess.

His chest heaved with each breath as rage fueled him on. With a cry much like a warrior, Riebl ran down the hall, his arms outstretched to clear the tops of any tables and to drive his knife into the faces of the unknown.

1 2

"No, no, don't even think about it!" Shayne Adams gripped the steering wheel hard with both hands, her knuckles turning white. "C'mon now, you wonderful piece of crap," she said as sweetly as she could through clenched teeth. "We're almost there. Just a few more miles to go. If you love me, you'll get us there." Shayne was rewarded with a loud popping sound, the clunking of gears of a dying engine, and everything mechanical in her blue 1991 Pontiac Grand Prix shutting down all at the same time.

A string of unpleasant words left her mouth making her sound more like a sailor than a sixteen-year-old girl. She eased the car to the side of the road, stomped on the brake, jammed the gear shift into park and threw open the driver's side door. She stood watching as smoke billowed out from under her closed hood, her mouth gaping open.

"Really?" she yelled. "There was maybe three miles to go! You couldn't give me three stinkin miles?" She began kicking the nearest tire only to be awarded, once again, with a loud pop and her tire to deflate.

She looked up at the sky and began to count to no specific number. "How come I didn't see any of *this* coming?"

With frustration boiling through her blood, Shayne grabbed her cell phone and dialed the familiar number. She growled out a protest as it went to voice mail once again. Without leaving a message she angrily pushed the disconnect button and rechecked her phones GPS. "Three point two miles to go," she mumbled as she yanked her keys from the ignition, grabbed her bag, and slammed the door closed. Throwing her bag over her shoulder she began to count as she walked in the direction her GPS was telling her to go. "1,2,3..."

"Does it hurt?"

Teagan looked up into the sympathetic eyes of Maya. "No, it doesn't hurt."

"It looks as if you got it weeks ago," Rove said, taking her hand in his to pull her arm closer for a better look. "You got this after holding the sword?"

Teagan nodded.

"Any idea what it means?"

"Yes, actually. The Celtic knot means strength," Teagan began as Vlad came up behind her and placed his hands comfortingly on her shoulders. "There are several knots that mean the same thing. It's the design you have to look at. The more twists and turns the knot has, the more strength it provides to the person wearing it." She cleared her throat as her emotions began to surface and felt as Vlad's hands tightened. She knew what he was doing, preventing her from running. She had no intention of doing that. Not anymore.

"The sword going through the knot," Teagan paused pointing to it, "represents the Great Smith's sword, and the Griffon holding onto it all," she pointed to the golden eagle head on a lion's body with wings, "stands for vigilance and valiant soldier."

"And your sword..." Rune prompted.

"...is the Great Smith's sword."

"And the Great Smith is..." Rune asked, lifting his eyebrows and smiling.

Teagan laughed, the feel of it almost natural. "The Great Smith is a Celtic god. Whoever is chosen to hold this sword, and is worthy of its craftsmanship, the blade will never miss or dullen."

"That would explain why it broke for Riebl," Rove said, untwining his arms from across his chest. "May I?" he asked, pointing toward it.

Teagan shrugged. "Sure."

"You've seen this tattoo before, haven't you?" Roam asked, as Rove took the sword and stepped back from the group.

Teagan nodded. "Yes, my grandfather had one just like it."

"But not your dad?"

Teagan looked up into Roam's questioning eyes, "No. I've been thinking about that. It didn't make sense for my dad to be killed with this sword. He was supposed to be protected by it, not harmed, if he was a protector." She leaned back into Vlad and welcomed his comfort. "My grandfather took ill suddenly and passed away in his sleep when I was seven. I believe I was next in line to take possession of this sword. So when my grandfather died, I wasn't old enough to take over. I think my dad was chosen to only hold onto it until the day the sword was to choose me."

"Wow. It keeps pulling towards you."

Teagan stifled a laugh. Rove was standing with her sword in his two hands, his feet planted firmly apart. He was turning from side to side struggling to keep the sword in his grip, sweat beading on his forehead.

"Teagan is the sword's rightful owner," Adrianna interjected. "Now that it has attached to her, it is meant for only Teagan to hold. The more you fight with it, the more difficult the sword will be for you to hold it."

Rove stopped struggling, relief showed on his face when the sword became more manageable. "You say that as if the sword is alive."

"The sword is made of pure magic like Excalibur. So in many ways it is alive."

"Why does it seem so small?" Maya asked, reaching out to touch the sword. She drew her hand back when it wavered in Teagan's direction. "I would think, since it's a god's sword, that it would be larger. Like Excalibur."

Teagan reached out, accepting the sword back from Rove. "Because this sword was forged by a god, it is magical. Just like Adrianna said. It is able to realign itself for the person meant to hold it..." She struggled for a moment as thoughts of her dad and grandfather danced across her mind. She felt Rune's hand take her vacant one and she tightened their grip. "When my grandfather held this sword, and even my dad, it was longer and heavier. Almost the size of Excalibur."

"I don't remember you knowing all of this information before," Vlad said. "How do you know it now?"

Teagan shrugged. "When the sword claimed me, memories and knowledge returned. I didn't remember my training before. It must have been taken away when Riebl took the sword from my dad." Teagan felt the sword react from her anger so she quickly tamped it down. "I just wish it would've reminded me on how to put it away."

"Oh, that's easy," Adrianna replied, taking a few steps toward her. "You have to will it away."

Teagan lifted her eyebrows in response.

Adrianna laughed. "Securely hold your sword with both hands, Teagan. I'm going to bring out Excalibur and your sword will register it as a threat until you tell it otherwise."

"Wait!" Teagan panicked. "How do I tell my sword that?"

"By how you react to me and Excalibur. Say in your mind that we are not a threat, start doing that now." Adrianna raised her arms in front of her body, her hands placed as if they were already holding the sword. "Are you ready?"

Teagan took a breath, placed her feet apart, and securely held your sword with its tip pointing to the floor. "Ready."

As soon as Excalibur came into view, Teagan felt her sword react. Words invaded her mind telling her it was time to fight. The need to pull her sword apart came strongly, so strongly, it took over all reasoning in her mind making her forget everything Adrianna had just told her.

"Teagan."

She raised her eyes to look into Adrianna's green ones. "You have to believe I am not a threat or Excalibur and I will have to react until you do. Relax and believe, it will tell your sword the same."

Teagan inhaled a calming breath, relaxed her shoulders, her elbows and even her knees. She smiled at Adrianna welcoming her friendship and felt as the swords tip began to relax on the floor. She scooted back and sat next to Rune on the coffee table, but kept her hands securely on the hilt of her sword.

"Very good, Teagan, you learn quickly," Adrianna said. "Keep a firm hold now. I need to move Excalibur. Keep your thoughts pure. The sword may try to change your mind."

While Teagan thought over Adrianna's words, she watched as the boy's mother placed Excalibur across both of her upturned hands. She felt the sword in her mind, but didn't listen to it, repeating to herself that there was no threat here. Adrianna lifted her hands so her arms were straight out in front of her body, Excalibur gleaming in all its glory.

"There is no threat here, be gone until I need you again," Adrianna said quietly but firmly. With a stir of the air, Excalibur lifted from her upturned hands and disappeared.

She turned, smiling at Teagan. "Once you get the hang of it, it's as easy as breathing. Now it's your turn."

Teagan nodded, slowly standing from the coffee table. She felt Rune's hand travel down her back making her anxiety lessen.

"Take your sword and lay it across your palms as I did," Adrianna instructed, demonstrating with her now empty hands. "You have to be confident, Teagan, or your sword will feel your unease and make this difficult for you. Once you get the hang of it, and your sword recognizes you as the one in charge, you will be able to will it away right from your grasp."

Teagan felt her cheeks redden. She bit down on her lower lip and stepped away from Rune. She would never be able to forgive herself if he was hurt again. She placed the sword across her palms as instructed, and looked to Adrianna.

"You're doing great, Teagan," Adrianna said. "Now, I don't tell Excalibur out loud anymore when I don't need it. I did when I first started, when Merlin began teaching me. I want you to say it out loud so I can guide you if needed. Do you know what to say?"

"Yes," Teagan answered, planting her feet slightly apart and relaxing her shoulders. She thought in her mind of how everything was fine, and began to speak out loud just as Adrianna did. "There is no threat here, be gone until I need you again."

Nothing happened. Teagan fought with disappointment as she stared at the swords still in her grasp.

"You're doing fine. Try again with a little more force. *You* are the one in charge so prove it."

Teagan closed her eyes, inhaling through her nose and out her mouth. She visualized the sword in her grasp as words danced into her mind like a melody. She smiled as the words became known, making her feel confident and sure. "My fight is done. All is safe, so return to your rightful place." She felt a shift to the air and a tingling sensation travel up her arms, until no weight could be felt on her still upturned hands.

"You did it, Teagan," she heard Rune say quietly behind her.

Teagan looked up into Adrianna's eyes, smiled and dove into her arms just as the front doorbell rang.

"GOT IT!" Rove called over his shoulder while heading down the short hallway to the front door. He didn't know who he expected to find, but knew it wasn't this adorable, strawberry blonde haired girl not much taller than Teagan, looking slightly peeved. "Can I help you?" he asked, holding the door open with one hand.

He watched her frown turn into a smile, and well-defined dimples showed in her cheeks.

"Wow, I'm not being shown anything."

"Excuse me?"

The girl straightened her bag on her shoulder and checked her cell phone before answering in her slight southern drawl. "This is the Gustavo home, right?"

"Yeah." Rove leaned against the doorframe propping the door open with his foot and crossing his arms over his chest. "Who are you looking for?" She wasn't anyone from his school. He would've noticed her before.

The girl scratched her head and looked at him nervously. "Well, The King of the Night called my mama and gave her some info and directions..."

"I'm sorry," Rove interrupted. "The King of the Night?"

The girl laughed making Rove think it was the most magical sound he had ever heard. "That's what my mama calls Dracula. Is Vlad here?"

"Yeah, and you would be?"

"Shayne?" Teagan exclaimed from the end of the hallway. "What're you doing here?"

The girl peered into the doorway, a now full smile on her pretty face. "Teagan, thank goodness!" she answered placing a hand on his chest and looking at him from the corner of her eye.

Rove swallowed nervously, pushing the door open with his hand. He could swear he heard her say yum as she brushed past him under his extended arm.

"Thank you," she said, her cheeks slightly flushed. "Teagan, I've been trying to call you for hours! My car broke down three miles back that away."

Rove constrained a laugh. The way she indicated would put her in Maya's front yard.

"By the time I got here," Shayne continued, "I was one cranky mess. You can thank tall, dark, and yummy who opened the door for putting me in a better mood. Is he available by any chance?"

Rove leaned on the wall for support, feeling his cheeks turning red for probably the first time in his life.

"Well, well, well..." Rove heard in his mind. *"Do I see Mr. Tough blushing?"*

"Shut up, Rune," Rove replied silently, folding his arms over his chest and putting on his best glare.

Shayne turned, biting her bottom lip and looking at him. "Sorry, I always put my foot in my mouth and ramble on without thinking." She extended her right hand. "I'm Shayne Adams, friend of Teagan's. I'm sorry I embarrassed you and me in front of everyone."

Her cheeks blushed a darker shade of pink as Rove took her small hand in his. "Nice to meet you," he said, looking at her questionably.

"She heard you? Is she a vampire?" Maya asked telepathically.

"Yes, I can hear you and no, I am not a vampire," Shayne answered back telepathically as she dropped Rove's hand and moved more into the room to hug Vlad. Out loud, she added, "So don't go sharing your deepest secrets when I'm around because no one has figured out how to shut me out, and I can't close the telepathy door. I've tried."

"Bet she can't hear Roam," Rune said. "If he does his thing."

Rove stepped more into the room, watching as Shayne greeted his parents. "Yeah, give it a try, Roam."

Shayne turned, folding her arms over her chest and looked at him. His mouth suddenly went very dry.

"I have never in my life met triplets before and I can't believe how identical you are, but Teagan did tell me a little bit about you when we last spoke. Let's see if I get this right." She leaned into Vlad, looking completely comfortable being with the oldest and most ferocious vampire alive. "White streaks and easy going is Rune," Shayne said "Blue streaks and calm is Roam?" She smiled when Roam confirmed. She looked at Rove then and his body reacted in ways he didn't want. "That makes you Rove. Teagan says you're kinda a hot head. Red suits you." She averted her eyes and turned to Roam. "Go ahead. Give it your best shot."

Roam smiled, glancing in Rove's direction. *"Who is this girl who melts my brother's heart?"*

Laughter escaped Rune's lips, while Maya smacked Roam on the arm. Rove shifted nervously on his feet.

Shayne grabbed Teagan's arm when her friend stepped back. "You didn't hear him either?"

"I can never hear any of them, not even Rune."

"How'd you do it?" Shayne asked.

Roam shrugged. "A little gift from a prophecy. Apparently, when I want to, I can hear all but can't be heard."

"Ha!" Shayne said, placing an arm around Teagan's shoulders. "Very interesting." She turned around and looked at Rove with a mischievous grin. *"At least I can still hear you."*

Rove leaned heavily against the wall, placing his arms back across his chest and tried to look like he didn't care.

1 3

AN ODD CLUNKING SOUND WOKE MERLIN FROM A LIGHT SLEEP. HE BOLTED UP into a sitting position, staring out between the bars of his cell as a large picture frame crashed into the wall at the bottom of the steps. It wavered on its side before toppling over and breaking in half on the concrete floor. Shuffling footsteps with a loud thud followed, as well as a poor rendition of 'Henry the Eighth'. The singing got louder as the individual grew nearer until Riebl rounded the corner. He pulled something large and solid behind him, dragging it until he stopped directly in front of Merlin's cell.

"Well, well, well," he said, wiping sweat from his forehead with the back of his hand. "If it isn't the illustrious, Merlin the Wizard." Riebl pulled the heavy object to place in front of Merlin's cell, planting a foot on the head of a golden bust. "And, oh lookey here. So is this!" Riebl cackled with laughter, nearly falling over.

"Maybe you should come back when you're more yourself," Merlin stated, keeping a steady eye on his unwelcomed visitor.

"Stand up, ol' man," Riebl said, wiping his face with the bottom of his filthy black t-shirt. He looked at Merlin out of the corner of his eye. "I said stand up!"

Merlin stood, letting his arms dangle at his sides. He heard the unmistakable sound of a knife leaving its sheath, and Riebl's hand coming from the small of his back. How Merlin wished Kya hadn't bound his magic.

Riebl placed the knife's blade on the pointer finger of his left hand, leaning forward and putting his weight on his propped leg. His usually well-kept hair was in total disarray, falling into his eyes and looking straggly. "You know, I don't understand. Kya tells me to go after your grandson then she interrupts and..." he pauses, his cheeks flushing. "and...she gets *my* sword taken away!"

He stood, the point of the blade still on his finger, blood beginning to drip onto the cement floor. "*My* sword, gone...poof!" Riebl began to pace, his voice getting louder. "And then when I tell Kya to get it back, she tells me she can't. That it's meant for that short, spiky haired girl."

Interesting, Merlin thought. He continued watching Riebl with a keen eye.

"You know what I think?" Riebl grabbed onto the bars with one hand and stuck the blade between the bars with the other to point at him. "I think Kya's lying. Oh, she wants into the forbidden kingdom. No doubt about that. But she wants it all for herself. Well, you know what ol' man?" Riebl asked, blowing hair out his eyes.

Merlin swallowed, trying to avoid the urge to step back as he stared into the eyes of a vampire going insane.

Without waiting for an answer, Riebl smiled. "I'm going to stop Kya and you're going to help me."

This time Merlin did step back as Riebl drew away from the bars and cackled with laughter. He picked up the broken frame, pushed the ends together, and rested it against the bars of Merlin's cell.

"I brought this for you. Thought you'd enjoy the changes I made to it."

As Riebl left, his laughter echoing while he ascended the stairs, Merlin stared at his favorite portrait, now destroyed. He backed up until the backs of his legs touched his cement bed and he sat. He thought of words his grandson Rove would say, and with his eyes staring into the eyes of the golden bust said, "I am so screwed."

POSH STARED INTO THE MIRROR, her eyes tearing up as she looked at her own reflection. There was no mistaking it now. The whispers inside her head overtaking her thoughts were really there. She had been so careful when she had been on the inside with the insane Godard, and still she received the sickness. She let the tears fall as she sat on the side of the tub in the bathroom of the Gustavo home.

She didn't even remember how old she really was anymore. Not as old as Vlad, of course, but still centuries old. She had seen so much in her life, but at the same time, she felt as if she hadn't lived as much as she wanted. Before Teagan and the Gustavo boys, Vlad and his clan had lived dangerously, instilling the new laws in each and every vampire of not taking blood from humans or go insane, unless the humans asked of it. Posh hadn't taken blood from any human, but Godard had, the blood must've been transferred to her without her knowledge.

Only a little over a month ago, the Sorceress of the Sun had granted Vlad and his followers the ability to eat food and enjoy sunlight once again. How much Posh loved the warmth of the sun on her skin! She would sit for hours under its rays, drinking homemade lemonade and eating hot off the grill hot dogs with Diego and Teagan.

Teagan. The girl had lost so much already, how was she going to tell her this? Standing from the tub, Posh went to the sink and splashed cold water onto her face. As she reached for the hand towel, a plan developed inside her mind. Without a second thought, Posh left the bathroom, drawing her sunglasses out of her pocket and placing them over her eyes. Her idea would destroy her in the end, but so would the sickness. It was the only way to keep Teagan from suffering.

14

It was quiet now that Shayne had left with Teagan. Boy, that girl could talk! She mixed sentences together so fast you didn't have time to catch up. Rune hooked his thumbs in his front pockets and smiled. Shayne was going to stir up a lot of feelings around here, and those feelings were Rove's.

"Nice night."

Rune jumped, turning to see Rove smiling behind him, his hands stuffed into the front pocket of his black jeans, his thumbs exposed. "Gee, Rove, how about a little warning next time?"

"How about you pay more attention than dreaming about your girlfriend? If Kya or Riebl had shown up instead of me, you'd be one hurting unit."

Rune nodded, looking over to the tree house and its large gaping hole. "The way they seem to keep out of my radar, you're probably right. And I wasn't dreaming about Teagan."

"Maybe you should be." Roam's voice said before he appeared at the side of the house from walking Maya home. He stopped when he reached the debris left in the yard and moved it with his foot. "That power of yours sure can pack a punch." Roam lifted his head to look at his youngest brother. "You were with Teagan when this happened. I was with Maya when she took out the rogue vamps. Maybe this is how it is meant to be. Me with Maya, you with Teagan...."

"...and Rove with Shayne." Rune finished, turning his head to look at his oldest identical brother. Rove stopped his fist mid-swing when he looked back at Rune.

"You're not kidding," he said nervously, his face looking like he was about to get sick.

"It makes sense," Roam interjected. "We're fighting a battle here, a battle that was foretold before we were even born. Our powers need to be stronger than theirs to win this thing."

"The prophecy didn't say anything about girls," Rove spouted back. "It only stated about us and Maya. There was no mention of Teagan, or....another girl."

"Her name is Shayne," Rune replied, smiling. It was kind of fun to see his oldest, tough-as-nails brother sweat.

"Don't say her name," Rove replied through gritted teeth. "She might hear you and come back. I don't need the girl hanging all over me."

Roam laughed. "Shayne has really gotten under your skin. I don't think I've ever seen you sweat over a girl."

"I'm not sweating over a girl," Rove retorted. "She just...well she kind of scares me."

Rune roared with laughter. "You, afraid of a girl?"

"She's pretty blunt, you know," Rove answered. He ran his hand through his hair, his red streaks spiking up under the porch light.

"You mean, like you?" Roam laughed. "I think you've finally met your match and you don't know what to do about it."

"She's also very pretty," Rune added, side-stepping away from Rove.

"She's a knock-out." Rove rocked back on his heels. "But why now? Whatever happened to getting to know someone first?"

"Haven't you heard of love at first sight?" Rune jumped off the porch only to be tackled by Rove mid-jump. He landed hard on his side onto the ground, the air leaving his lungs with a whoosh. Rove shoved him onto his back and straddled him, sitting on his stomach as Roam laughed.

"Hmmm...let's see," Rove began, a cocky grin on his face. "To breathe or not to breathe?"

Rune sipped in a small amount of air. "To love or not to love." The pressure built as Rove put all his weight on his stomach before standing up. Rune rolled onto his side gasping and laughing at the same time.

"Hey, what's that?" Roam bent down next to him to pick something off the ground. Rune flopped onto his back to see Roam standing with the necklace he had found in the cave dangling from his fingers.

"Found it...in the cave," Rune gasped out. "Kept meaning to show you guys...but kept forgetting...with all these girls showing up and all."

Rove play-kicked him in the leg, then reached a hand down to help him to his feet.

"When did you find this in the cave?" Roam asked, turning it in his fingers.

"During our party when I went to go get the cookies."

Rove grasped the compressed washer in-between his fingers. "You stopped at the cave when you went to go get cookies?"

"After I went to get cookies," Rune corrected, stuffing his hands into the back pockets of his cargo shorts.

"Why?" Roam questioned.

"Because when I flew overhead I felt this pull, so on the way back I stopped."

Rove let the necklace slip from his fingers to dangle from Roam's. He crossed his arms across his chest. "You felt a pull at the cave and you went in by yourself?"

"I scanned it before I landed for threats. There wasn't any, so I went in. And I scanned a second time when I was inside, leaving feelers out while I was there. What's the big deal?"

"What's the big deal?" Rove leaned forward getting into Rune's face. "Remember the last time you scanned for threats and Roam almost died?"

Rune rocked back on his heels, "I...didn't think about that."

"You didn't think about that?" Rove repeated getting louder. "What is wrong with you?"

"Hold on," Roam interrupted, stepping between them. He placed a hand on Rove's chest making him take a step back. "We're not going to get anywhere if we fight amongst ourselves." He looked to both of his brothers. "We good?"

Rune nodded, stepping back and staring at the blades of grass at his feet.
"We need to make a pact."

Rune looked up to find Rove looking directly at him. "None of us goes into any place that doesn't feel right, off, strange, or out of the ordinary without the others. Agreed?" He lifted his hand between them sticking out his pinkie finger.

Rune stared at it. Pinkie swearing was something their mom had done with them when they were little. Roam interlocked his pinkie with Rove's.

"Deal?" Rove asked.

"Yeah, deal," Rune agreed, adding his own pinkie and squeezing.

"Now that we have that taken care of, let's take a closer look at this necklace." Roam grabbed the compressed washer, bringing it up to his eye. "There has to be a reason you found this. Give me some light, Rune."

Rune made an orb appear and held it up above their heads.

"There's something written or stamped here," Roam said, holding it more into the light Rune's orb made.

"I noticed that too but I forgot to take a closer look at it when I got home."

"Just like you forgot to mention it and your little stop to us," Rove replied, smacking Rune upside the head. "Start using your brain, Rune, before you get caught up in something and we're not there to save your butt."

"Lighten up, Rove," Roam demanded, still looking at the necklace. "Kya's looking for a breaking point and if you two keep it up she'll have what she needs to take us all out."

"Can you tell what's stamped on it or not?" Rove asked, irritated, crossing his arms and puffing out his chest.

Roam turned away, walking towards one of the planks that had broken free from the wall laying in the yard. He palmed the necklace with his left hand and raised his right. "Let's see if this works," he said as blue lightning shot from his hand, dancing across his fingertips. Rune looked to Roam's face and saw the determination, until the lightening was one lone streak shooting out of his pointer finger.

"Awesome." The lightning took on a laser pointer kind of effect, but with much more power. Rune walked around to the other side of the board, squinting at lines and squiggles permanently burning into the wood. He frowned and had no idea what his brother was drawing. When Roam was done, he lowered his hand and took a step back. Rove came to stand next to Roam, his hands on his sides.

"Some kid just made squiggly lines?" Rove asked, turning his head in different directions looking at it.

"I think it's a word," Roam answered.

Rune moved to another corner to get a different perspective, a frown still on his face. "r...e...g?...d...o...?"

"No, I think it's an i not a g," Rove corrected.

"That's not an i. Everything else is lower-case. I think it's a cl," Roam added.

"So, r...e...c...l...d...o?" Rune recited. He was getting disappointed. Here he was led to something and it was turning out to be nothing.

"That's not a word." Rove moved the board so it was facing him. "I think something is missing. Check it again, Roam."

"That's all I see, but it's in a type of cursive so maybe I missed something. Maybe you should look at it." He handed the necklace off to Rove who squinted at it and handed it off to Rune.

"Maybe it will bring you good luck?"

"Nothing wrong with good luck," Rune answered. He withdrew his own necklace from under his shirt and removed it. He slipped the compressed washer onto the chain with the silver crescent moon and sun marking him as a Gustavo vampire, a necklace they all wore. Pleased with the effect, he stuffed it back under his t-shirt and followed his brothers into the house.

BLACKNESS SWIRLED across the dungeon floor beginning to take on form until falling apart to swirl again. Kya's palms slapped down on the tabletop. She was close, she could feel it. What was she missing? She yanked the book of black magic forward, tucking a stray, red curl behind an ear.

'How to Make an Army' was written in bold across the top of the page in Latin. She ran her fingernail down the script until she found what she had missed. Leaving her fingernail in place, she drew a smaller book down and opened it, carefully leafing through its weathered pages until she found the words she needed to decipher. She reread it three times before a bubble of laughter began deep in her stomach. It was almost comical what the words translated into. Not able to contain it anymore, Kya threw her head back, splaying her arms wide as deep laughter escaped her lips.

All she was missing was the blood of a high-ranking wizard.

1 5

TEAGAN SMILED AS SHAYNE SPOKE ON HER CELL PHONE TO HER MOM AS THEY made their way to the Gustavo home. The sun was shining brightly in a cloudless sky, with a light breeze blowing making the air seem cooler than it really was. It was going to be the hottest day so far, a whopping eighty-five degrees with low humidity. Teagan's favorite kind of weather.

"Mama says hi," Shayne said, swiping a finger across the screen of her iphone and stuffing it into the front pocket of her shorts, her flip-flops making a smacking sound as she walked. "She says she'll pay the Gustavos for looking at my car. I keep telling her I need a new one and she just keeps saying, 'Shayne girl, you need to learn the importance of the dollar and appreciating what you do have.' I keep telling her I do appreciate it, but the car just doesn't appreciate me." She stopped suddenly looking around. "Where are we? Everything looks the same in these woods."

"The Gustavo home is just ahead," Teagan answered with a laugh.

"What's so funny?" Shayne asked, placing her hands on her hips.

"You," Teagan answered. "You ramble on when you're nervous."

"I'm not nervous," Shayne answered. "I'm just over-excited to see tall, dark and yummy."

"Then why are your cheeks turning red?"

Shayne rolled her eyes and let out a puff of air. "Okay, I didn't make the greatest impression last night and probably scared off triplet number three. But the vision didn't show any of them and how gorgeous they are and I got thrown off a little."

"Rove is triplet number one," Teagan corrected. "Rune is number three. What vision? You didn't tell me about a vision."

"Really?" Shayne answered, smiling. "The oldest, huh? Guess that makes sense." Shayne looked down at the ground dragging the toe of her flip-flop in the dirt. She looked up when Teagan loudly cleared her throat and folded her arms across her chest. "Oh, all right. I had this strange vision. There was this woman with long red hair wearing this gorgeous black dress, and some guy with long black hair and a red tint in his eye."

Teagan felt the color drain from her face. "Shay, what else did you see?"

Shayne squinted. "You know who I'm talking about don't you?"

Teagan wet her lips. "Yes. Now tell me what else you saw then I will tell you who they are."

"All I saw was the red-haired, evil looking woman laughing and the long haired guy looking scared. The red head raised her hands, and this black goo looking stuff traveled out from underneath her magnificent looking dress and began to take on the form of a person. Then I saw you and I woke up."

Teagan bit her lower lip. "Maybe we should meet up with the boys, tell them what you saw, and then we can all fill you in on what you don't know."

"No, no, no, Teags," Shayne said, wagging her finger. "You said if I told you about the vision, you would tell me who they are. Now spill, girl."

Teagan sighed loudly. "The red haired, crazy woman is named Kya and she is a sorceress. The black haired vampire is Riebl. They are both a pain in the butt and want us all dead."

Shayne's mouth fell open. "They want you all dead? Why you? You just got here, what could you have possibly done?"

"The sword Riebl was using turned out to be mine."

"What?" Shayne asked. "What do you mean yours?"

"Don't freak out Shay, okay?" Teagan asked, just seconds before her sword magically appeared in her left hand. She looked sheepishly at Shayne's terrified face.

"What the freak is that?" Shayne exclaimed, taking a step backward.

"The Great Smith's sword," Teagan answered. "I'm its protector." She shifted the sword into her right hand and showed Shayne the tattoo on the inside of her left wrist. "Don't worry. It won't hurt you," Teagan said as Shayne backed up more.

"*It* won't hurt me?" Shayne questioned incredulously. "You mean it attacks on its own?"

"It's magical," Teagan answered, "It...it speaks to me."

"It speaks to you," Shayne repeated throwing her arms into the air then letting them drop to slap her thighs. "I thought we said we'd lose our minds together when we were old and frail."

Teagan laughed. "It speaks to me because it's magically forged by a god. When there's a threat it encourages me."

"You mean to tell me that sword sees me as a threat and is telling you to attack me?" Shayne asked, pointing at herself.

"No," Teagan answered, waving her free hand. "That's how it works. It's not viewing you as a threat. I'd never hurt you."

"What is going on?" Shayne complained, looking upward. "First, I'm not shown any of the Gustavo boys or Maya. Then you become the benefactor of a lethal sword? Why isn't my premonition power working?"

"Maybe you weren't supposed to see it. Maybe this is how you were supposed to find out."

"It's a little disconcerting," Shayne replied. "Can you put that thing away? You're scaring the crud out of me."

With silent words, the sword vanished. Teagan stood, her hands clasped in front of her body looking at her best friend. "Are you mad?"

Shayne looked at her questioningly. "Why would I be mad at you?"

Teagan shrugged. "You weren't shown any of this and I freaked you out."

Shayne put her arm around Teagan's shoulders, beginning to walk. "That's not your fault, girl. I'm thinking I'm not supposed to see everything. Otherwise, where would the fun be in being surprised?"

HE COULD SENSE them long before he saw them. Rune closed their large book and stood up from the deck chair he was sitting on, putting on a smile.

"They're here, aren't they?" Rove grumbled from the chair next to Rune's, his feet propped up on the deck table.

"Yup," Rune answered with a chuckle.

"It's not funny," Rove complained. He slapped his notebook closed and tossed it over his feet, missing the tabletop. He hissed as it landed on the deck.

"Oh, really?" Rune asked, reaching down and retrieving the notebook to place it on the table. "So it was okay for you to give me a hard time, but it's not okay for me to do it to you?"

"Touché," Rove replied. "How are we supposed to find this book and key if these girls keep popping out of the woods to distract us?"

Rune laughed, "Maybe it's because the girls are supposed to be here. And maybe Shayne..."

"Don't you dare finish that sentence," Rove threatened pointing a finger at him.

Rune snickered, turning to watch as Teagan stepped out of the woods. He felt the flutter in his chest the minute her eyes locked onto his. Yup, he was done for.

"How long ago did you know we were coming?" Teagan asked as Shayne spotted Rove and grinned, her adorable dimples concaving in her cheeks.

"Oh, ten minutes ago?" Rune guessed as Shayne came to stand at the bottom of the deck, her eyes still on Rove.

"Good morning, handsome," she drawled. "Aren't you bright eyed and handsome already this morning."

Rove sneered at her before diverting his attention to Teagan. "Good morning, Finn. I see you brought short, red and annoying with you."

"Finn? Her name is Teagan. And my hair isn't red, it's strawberry blonde."

Rove re-crossed his ankles and pointed at Teagan. "Her last name is Finnegan isn't it, Red?"

"Don't call me that," Shayne said stepping up onto the deck to stand in front of Rove. "My name is Shayne, that's it. No nickname or derogatory remarks. As long as you remember that, we'll get along just fine."

"Okay," Rove said, his feet hitting the deck with a slap. He stood up, crossing his arms across his chest and towering over Shayne's five-foot-two frame. "My name is Rove, not handsome, yummy or any other derogatory name or remark. Do you always meet new people and become an instant thorn in their side?"

"Do you always get into people's faces and argue about every little thing?" Shayne asked, placing a hand on her hip and staring Rove straight in the eye.

Rune put his arm around Teagan's shoulders and pulled her close. Rove had finally met his match. "This is better than going to the movies."

"As a matter of fact, yes." Rove continued. "You always move your head like that and speak as if you're a relative of Whoopi Goldberg?"

Shayne smiled. "As a matter of fact, yes. My mama's black. You got a problem with that?"

Rove's eyebrows raised. "*Your* mama's black?"

"Yes, I'm adopted. My papa is white and mama is black." Shayne took one step closer. "You got a problem with inter-racial couples?"

"Whoa," Rove demanded, putting his hands up palms out. "Don't turn me into some kind of bigot."

"Pig-headed he is," Rune interjected with a laugh. "Bigot he is not."

"Thanks, bro," Rove said, reaching over with his fist to knuckle bump his brother.

Shayne glanced in Teagan's direction, then down at her flip-flops. "Sorry, didn't mean to spout that out."

"Huh," Rove spurted back. "An apology, look at that."

Shayne's eyes lifted and Rune felt Teagan stiffen. "I do know when to apologize when I am out of line. You, on the other hand, can't quit while you're ahead."

"Well, as long as we have that straight."

Teagan pried herself away and Rune felt empty without her standing next to him. He watched as Teagan grabbed Shayne by the arm and pulled her into the yard. No lips were moving so Rune knew that at least Teagan was speaking telepathically to Shayne.

Rove came to stand next to him, hooking his thumbs into the front pocket of his jeans. "What do you think's happening?"

"I'm thinking the two of you should probably stay away from each other until you can play nice."

"Got no complaint from me on that," Rove answered.

Rune could see Shayne responding to Teagan, but still couldn't hear what Teagan was saying to Shayne. "You think Roam could hear what was being said if he were here?"

"Absolutely," Rove answered, nodding. "Do you think it's important that we know what's being said?"

"Maybe," Rune murmured. He tried to reach out to Teagan, but again he found the door to her thoughts completely closed. "It might help us to understand Shayne a little better."

"And we need to know about her because..."

"Like it or not, Rove, Shayne's here for a reason. I'm sure about that. Just like Teagan is here for a reason."

Rove rocked on his heels, letting out a huff of air. "I don't want someone else setting me up with the person I might be meant to be with."

Rune turned to look at his brother. "Is that what you're afraid of?"

Rove nodded. "Yeah, that's what I'm afraid of." He stared out at the girls. "I mean, Roam fell for Maya. You fell for Finn, and..."

Rune raised his eyebrows. "And..."

Rove swore, turning around to face Rune, his back to the girls. He took a deep breath through his nose. "The minute I saw that girl I knew." He dragged his hand through his hair, his foot lightly tapping on the deck. "You're not laughing."

"Nothing funny to laugh at," Rune said considerately. "Don't think of Shayne being here for you. Instead, think about why she is here. Let everything else fall to the wayside. But in the meantime, you're going to have to find a way to get along with her. We really don't know how much time we have to find this book and key Kya wants. We can't get Pappy back if we don't work together."

"When did you get so smart?" Rove asked, smirking.

"When I stopped being afraid about Teagan," Rune answered.

"Why do you have the word recludo burned into this board?"

Rune and Rove turned at the same time to see Shayne and Teagan standing over the board Roam had carved into last night.

"What did you say?" Rove asked.

"Why do you have recludo burned into this board?" Shayne repeated, pushing the board with her foot.

"Recludo? You can read that?" Rune questioned. "It's a word?"

"Yeah. It's Latin, it means to open or unlock."

Rune looked over at Rove and swallowed nervously.

Rove placed his hand firmly on Rune's shoulder before looking back at Shayne. "You're sure that's what it says?" he asked uncertainly.

"Yeah, I am," Shayne answered, cocking her head and squinting at Rove. "Why do you look like I just fed someone their death sentence?"

"Because you just might have. Come on in. We have a lot to talk about."

16

"WHAT BOOK IS THAT?" MERLIN SAT UP STRAIGHTER ON HIS HARD BED, HIS interest piqued. Riebl had been rambling on and on for what seemed like an hour complaining about Kya. Nothing that Merlin found interesting in the least until the nightwalker mentioned a book.

Riebl shrugged one shoulder while flipping his knife between his fingers. "It's a big, black book with a carved upside down star on the cover. When she opens it, she has to burn two black candles and one white one. She says the black ones are to open the black magic it contains." Riebl waved his fingers in mockery. "When I was playing with the flame of the white candle she said if I put it out, we would get sucked into the book and live the rest of our lives in hell."

Merlin could feel the blood drain from his face. "Where does she keep this book, Riebl?"

Riebl leaned back on the bust he was using as a seat, crossing an arm over his chest and pointing the tip of his knife at Merlin. "Why do you want to know?"

Merlin stood, grasping onto the bars of his cell. "It's important. Where is the book?"

Riebl stood, walking the length of the cell with his eyes on Merlin. "I'm not sure if I should tell you that," he finally answered.

"Would you bring it then and show it to me?"

Riebl spun, rushing to where Merlin stood and grasping one of the bars with his free hand. "Are you crazy? I'm not touching that book, nor would I allow you to touch it. You'd probably vaporize me with one of its spells!"

Merlin thought of mentioning Kya would probably do that, but decided against it. "I only want to see it, Riebl. I want to know if it's the one I think it is."

"Why?"

Merlin didn't know if he should tell this vampire the truth. He was treading on dangerous ground as it was and if Kya found out...

"I asked you why ol' man."

Merlin looked up to find Riebl's knife tip inches from his eye. "If that book is the one I think it is," Merlin responded carefully, "It is sacred and very dangerous. If that book is the one I think it is, Kya is in grave danger."

Riebl snorted, lowering his knife and taking a step back. "Wouldn't that be in your favor?"

"No," Merlin responded, rolling his shoulders in relief. "It puts us all in danger. Using black magic has consequences, Riebl, and it's not picky as to who has to pay the price."

Riebl placed his hand on his hip, knife blade pointing down. "What do you want to do with it?"

"I can't do anything with it," Merlin answered, holding up his arms to show his bound wrists. "But I can tell you how to get rid of it."

"I told you, I'm not touching that book."

"Then let me out," Merlin begged. "I'll tell you how to get rid of these binds of magic and I'll destroy the book!"

Riebl backed up, shaking his head from side to side. "I'm not falling for your tricks, ol' man," he said, rounding the corner and sprinting up the stone steps.

Merlin closed his eyes and rested his forehead on the bars. They were all in deeper trouble than he thought. He had to find a way out.

ROVE LEANED against the doorway from the kitchen watching Rune stare out the living room window, while his parents prepared lunch behind him. If Shayne was right with her definition, Rune had a lot to be worried about.

"Did you get a hold of Roam?" his dad asked.

"I had to call Maya's cell," Rove responded, his eyes still on Rune. "They should be here in fifteen minutes."

"We'll keep Rune safe, Rove."

"I know, Dad," he replied. "Whatever it takes I'm making sure he is." Pressure suddenly built, bearing weight down on his chest making him want to lash out. He hated it when his emotions got the better of him.

"Rove?" A small hand touched the middle of his back and he nearly jerked away when his heart did a flip-flop in his chest. "I just want to say if you need anything you only need to ask."

"You could take back what you said outside," he suggested, still watching Rune. He felt Shayne's arm come around his waist nearly making him jump out of his skin.

"If I could I definitely would," Shayne answered.

Rove turned, he felt Shayne's arm leave his back and he realized he wished it were still there. "What if..."

Shayne raised her eyebrows, cocking her head to the side. "What if...what?"

Rove grabbed her hand and pulled her past his parents and right out the back door. Once outside he turned to face her straight on. "What if you're wrong?"

"But I'm not wrong," Shayne argued, placing her hands on her hips.

He ran a hand through his hair, turning and walking to the end of the deck facing the woods. He hooked his thumbs in his front pockets, rocking back on his heels. "You mean to tell me you can read Latin?" He felt her hand on his back again and grimaced. "Please don't touch me."

Shayne's hand stilled on his back. "Why not?"

"Because..." Rove sighed, his head falling back. "Because you make me feel."

Shayne kept her hand on his back and patted his stomach with her other. "Why is that a bad thing?"

"Because I don't want to have feelings for you right now," he answered his voice tight. He felt her body brush his as she came to stand in front of him. She pried his thumbs out his pockets and clasped his hands with both of hers.

"Look at me, Rove," she demanded squeezing his hands.

Rove dragged his eyes down from the trees to look into her gray eyes, and couldn't help but think how beautiful they were. "What?" he asked agitated.

"You need to let go."

Rove looked at her questioningly. "You're the one holding my hands."

She smiled and Rove felt a layer of stress fall away when her dimples flashed. "You need to let go of what's tearing you up inside. I don't know why I have strong feelings for you, but I do. I just want to help you get through whatever my findings have done to make you and your brother so upset."

Emotions were something Rove never made time for, they generally ticked him off. But tears welled up in his eyes anyway making him bite his bottom lip.

"Oh, isn't this sweet. Quality time with the girlfriend instead of finding my book and key."

Shayne's upper arm was grabbed and before she knew it, she was spinning around and smacking into Rove's back narrowly missing smashing her nose.

"Let go of me!" Shayne demanded, trying to yank her arm free from Rove's secure grasp.

"Get out of here, Kya. You're not welcome here!" Rove snarled as Rune suddenly materialized next to them.

"Whoa," Rune gasped, wavering on his feet until he seemed to get his bearings. He planted his feet apart, shook his head, and brought his hands in front of his body palms up orbs appearing in each hand.

"How...?" Rove began.

"Later," Rune answered as the back door flung open and Teagan and the boys' parents spilled out.

Wanting to see what was going on Shayne stopped pulling and peered under Rove's arm. She couldn't help but stare as fire danced on Rove's rope all the way up to his elbow. Both of Rune's hands were holding some kind of white orb with something swirling inside of them. She was even more amazed when her best friend's sword appeared, and watched as Teagan grabbed the sword with both hands and pulled it apart to make two.

"Oh, come now. I only want to chat."

Shayne diverted her eyes from Teagan to look at the woman from her vision in the yard. She was walking the length of the deck, her long, red, curling hair trailing down the back of an ugly medieval, emerald dress. The bottom of Kya's dress was swaying with blackness oozing out from underneath, spreading across the grass and beginning to climb up onto the deck.

"What do you want, Kya?"

Shayne's eyes popped as she stared at Adrianna moving alongside her husband to the front of the deck with the most magnificent looking sword she had ever seen. They stopped next to Rove while Kya turned a questioning look on her beautiful, evil face, pointing with one long, black fingernail first at Rove, then at Rune.

"There's a brother missing," she said smiling. "Where is he?"

"Where's your vampire on a leash?" Rove retorted.

Kya cocked her head and bowed slightly. "Well played."

As soon as Shayne felt Rove loosen his grip, she pulled her arm out of his grasp and came to stand next to him, jutting her chin out as she looked at Kya.

"Get back behind me," Rove ordered telepathically.

"No."

"Please?" Even telepathically, Shayne could tell Rove was asking through gritted teeth.

"I have no intention of leaving your side," she answered silently, her eyes still on Kya. *"What if you need your other hand? You can't hold me and your rope thingy at the same time."*

Shayne heard a huff come from Rove just seconds before a second rope materialized in his empty hand. He snapped it, angrily bringing it to flame. The flames extended up both arms making him look like a stunt man in a burning building. He took a step closer to Kya. *"Don't move, Shayne,"* he ordered telepathically. "Last chance, Kya," Rove called loudly. "What do you want?"

"I merely wanted to check on your progress of..." Her voice faltered as Roam and Maya landed on the deck between Rove and Rune.

Shayne felt like she was in a paranormal movie with all of them standing majestically with powers she had never seen before. Fire, electricity, and a bright whiteness intermixed around a purple haze, which seemed to float on the outermost layer. She could hear the brothers and Maya speaking telepathically to each other, but not Teagan. Her best friend stood next to Rune with her eyes trained on the threat in the yard. Her hands were in front of her body holding the two swords as if she had carried them all her life, her tattoo glowing. Shayne took a few steps back when she heard what the boys were going to do. She quickly relayed the message to Teagan then looked back at Kya. She didn't want to miss a thing.

Kya stopped, her eyes staring, her head tilting to the side. A mixture of surprise and disbelief crossed her face as she continued to stare at Maya. She turned her hands palm up at her sides, her fingers curling back, her long nails almost touching each other as she turned her surprised gaze to Teagan. She staggered backward almost as if she was hit with a sudden realization, when her gaze shifted to Shayne and lingered.

Feeling uncomfortable, Shayne moved forward as Rove stepped back, neither of them taking their eyes off the sorceress standing in the flattened green grass in the yard. Standing as close as she could to Rove, Shayne could feel the power emanating from him causing a tingling sensation to travel up her arm next to his. She could hear the boys communicating with each other, discussing if they should attack while she was otherwise engaged. Kya's eyes seemed to grow wider as she snarled, anger replacing surprise. With a jerking, aggressive motion, Kya lifted one hand up, twisted it and disappeared.

Rove suddenly spun around, frantically slapping and patting her arms. "Are you okay?" he said a little too loudly.

"Yeah," Shayne nodded, slowly turning her gaze from where Kya had been in the yard to look into Rove's concerned face. "Yeah, I'm fine. Stop smacking me!"

"You're sure?" He was holding her hands, ignoring her request. He twisted her arms back and forth with his mom standing next to him, peering at her arms. "Did I burn you?"

Shayne was confused. "What? What do you mean did you burn me?" She looked down to see the last of the residual flames evaporate. "So, that's what I felt," she mumbled as everyone else surrounded them.

"You're really okay?"

Shayne looked into Rove's terrified face and grabbed onto his hands. "Rove, I'm fine. Honest."

"You don't look fine," Teagan interjected. "You look scared."

Shayne looked from one to the next before she finally said, "Does anyone else think Kya looked at me as if I wasn't supposed to be here?"

Rove swore and pulled her to his chest. She felt his hand on the back of her head as he held her securely. "We need to find the book and key she wants now," Rove ordered. "This little masquerade needs to be done."

For the first time in a long time, Shayne had nothing to add. She grasped onto Rove tighter burying her face in his chest and smiled.

17

An annoying tapping sound brought Merlin out of his deep meditation. He was sitting on his stone bed with his legs crossed and his hands resting comfortably on his thighs. A sigh of unease escaped his lips when he looked up to see Kya walking the length of his cell running her fingernails across the bars. She showed no signs of discomfort, or even acknowledgment, when her bare feet padded over his destroyed portrait.

"I wonder how you did it," Kya asked as she walked past him, her fingernails still tapping across the bars. "I mean, you're in there. So you must have done it before."

"What is it that I presumably did?" Merlin questioned, his eyes watching her as she stopped in front of him to turn back the way she started.

Kya snickered, looking back over her shoulder at him. "You really want me to believe that you don't know what I'm talking about?"

"Kya, I assure you..."

"The Sisters of the Realm," she interrupted, her eyes trained on his as she spoke. "How did you bring together the Sisters of the Realm?"

"The Sisters of the Realm are a myth," Merlin answered, scrunching his eyebrows together. "Nothing more, nothing less. There is no proof they even exist."

Kya circled back, the bottom of her dirty emerald dress swaying at her ankles and her eyes challenging his. "*You* are nothing more than a myth to the general population of the world. And yet, here you are in the flesh." She grabbed onto the bars. Her long, black nails protruding outward, her eyes latched onto his as she spoke in a slow, clipped tone. "There are three girls at your granddaughter's home. One with each of your grandsons. One blonde, one brunette, and one red."

"Surely you don't think..."

"Oh, yes. I do think," Kya interrupted sternly. She smiled, stepping back from the bars and flicking her right wrist making a standard sized book appear already opened to a specific page. "'The Sisters of the Realm,'" she read loudly, looking over the book at him then back down at the pages. "'Born of a Goddess and a mortal, these sisters will be deemed the Sisters of the Realm. One as bright as the sun, one the flame of the horizon, and one as dark as midnight. They are the only magical beings who can open and close the gateway at will to grant access to those who are deserving, and banish those who are not.'"

"And you think these girls with my grandsons are the Sisters of the Realm?"

"Don't play smug with me, Merlin," Kya scoffed. "You found them and set them up with your grandsons. You did this."

Merlin ran his fingers down his tangled beard. "Kya, are you aware of the Sorcerer's Oath?"

She splayed her fingers in front of her in mocked shock. "Duh! Of course I am!"

"Then you know a sorcerer or sorceress can never blatantly lie or be punished in the most horrible of ways." Merlin clasped his hands in front of his body. "I swear to you, Kya, I do not know who the other two girls are at the home of my granddaughter."

"Ah, but there is a loophole in your Oath," she said wagging a finger in his direction. "If you lie to protect the good then you are forgiven. And let's face it, you work for good and I work with evil intentions in mind, so your point is moot."

She was right of course. "I assure you Kya, I am not aware of who those two girls are. Nor have I knowingly brought together the Sisters of the Realm."

"Then you agree," Kya answered, pacing. "They *are* the Sisters of the Realm."

"No!" Merlin stated, exasperated. "I am merely stating if they are, I had nothing to do with it!"

Kya tapped her chin with one long fingernail, an evil looking smile spreading across her face. "At least there is one thing you can be held accountable for."

She crooked a finger at him and before Merlin knew what was happening, his body involuntarily moved toward the bars. There was nothing for him to grab onto as he was propelled toward Kya, to slam into the bars of his cell. Kya laughed as she reached inside and grabbed his right arm, pulling it through the space in the bars and pushing up his tattered sleeve to expose his forearm.

"I can't believe I just now remembered this most important detail," she said cheerfully as Merlin's eyes grew wide. She flipped his arm over to expose his inner arm. "Hold still now," Kya instructed. "This will only hurt a little."

Kya smiled, her eyes bright with craziness, as she drew a fingernail across his skin. Merlin cried out as a searing pain shot through his arm. Blood began flowing, trailing down his arm like branches of an old, gnarled tree. His blood dripped onto the cement floor until a small bottle appeared to magically float from drop to drop, to fill its emptiness to its brim.

"That will do just fine," Kya said, running her fingernail the opposite way across his skin closing his wound and letting go of his arm. "Don't want Riebl taking a taste, I might need you later." She laughed as she turned her back on him and waved. "Pleasure doing business with you!"

Merlin gaped at her retreating form, holding his arm protectively as the magic leaving his body burned. There was no turning back for Kya now. She was no longer dabbling with black magic. She *was* a mistress of black magic and there was no way for her to back out of it now. Fear bubbled up in his chest until he cried out in anger, letting tears fall down his cheeks to join droplets of his blood on the cement floor. Somehow, magic was going to allow him freedom and he demanded it let him know how!

"Alright, how'd you do it?" Rove leaned back against the counter, folding his arms over his chest and flicking red streaked hair out of his eyes.

"How'd who do what?" Roam asked, setting their large book on the counter and taking a seat on one of the high backed kitchen stools.

"How'd Rune materialize next to me and Shayne on the deck when Kya arrived?"

"You materialized?" Roam exclaimed, swiping blue streaked hair out of his eyes, only to have it return exactly as it had been. "How?"

Rune shrugged. "It happened the first time when I chased after Teagan. I said to myself how I wanted to stop her and suddenly I did."

"You teleported," Shayne said in awe, turning from leafing through the boys' book. "You've only done it twice? Why only twice? I thought you guys were wizards or something."

"We just got our powers," Rune answered, shaking his head and snickering at how Shayne could ask two questions in a row before he could answer the first. "It seems that whenever I get one under control another one appears."

"Although I'm not surprised and want to hear more about your new power," Dad stated, putting his arm around Mom's shoulders. "I'm concerned by Kya's interest in the girls, especially Shayne. I'm not sure if Kya was just confused by their presence or if there was recognition."

"Kya doesn't seem to know which one of us is which either," Rove pointed out, his gaze darting to Shayne and back again. Since Kya's arrival, he didn't let her too far from his sight. "All she knew is that one of us was missing. I think she thought Shayne was Maya up until Maya and Roam landed on the deck."

"Can't that go in our favor?" Rune asked opening the cupboard door and grabbing out a bag of pretzels. Using magic made him hungry.

"It could," Mom answered uncertainly. "At least with her not paying attention to you boys, but the girls? I'm not so sure. Shayne's right, I got the same impression she did. Kya was confused by you three girls. She appeared to look at Shayne knowingly, and with fear."

"I agree," Roam stated, taking Maya's hand in his. "She seemed frightened and angered by the three of you together. Whether Kya recognized Teagan or not, she and Maya were both here for the last battle. How about you, Shayne? You ever meet Kya before today?"

"Other than in my dream, no," Shayne answered, sticking her hand into the bag of pretzels and smiling at Rune as she popped one into her mouth.

"What do you mean in your dream?" Rove asked one eyebrow cocked.

Shayne gave a half smile as she chewed, glancing in Teagan's direction. "I sort of get premonitions while I'm sleeping. It's what brought me here."

"What exactly did you see?" Roam asked.

"I saw Kya in a beautiful black dress," Shayne answered while playing with the pretzels in her hand. "With the same blackness that came out from under it as today, but it formed into a kind of person. Then I saw Teagan and woke up."

"How often do your premonitions come true?" Rove questioned, inching closer to her.

"Every time," Shayne replied sheepishly, leaning back against the counter and smiling uneasily up at Rove. He reached into her hand and stole a pretzel, never taking his eyes off her.

"I haven't seen a black dress yet," Maya said, looking at Roam for confirmation. "When we do we have to be prepared."

"I'm going to stress to you girls, no matter how much power and magic any of you have, you need to stay close. I'm uncomfortable with Kya and her reaction," Mom said with concern.

"But I don't have any powers," Shayne answered. "Other than premonitions."

"Premonitions can be an extremely important source of power," Mom interjected. "Don't take your power lightly, Shayne."

Shayne nodded while Rove threw an arm over her shoulders.

Mom smiled. "Maya, call your parents and have them pack a bag. I want them here within the hour. Teagan, I want you to stay here, and Shayne I want you to call your parents and ask them if you can stay for a time. Sending you home would not be safe for you or your family. We found that out the first time too late and Maya's parents were hurt mentally and physically."

"My parents have decided to visit my aunt in Ohio," Maya mentioned, returning her cell phone to her pocket. "They'd like some help in packing so they can leave quickly. I would like them to have some lookouts until they are safely on the highway."

"Rove and I can head over with Maya," Roam said, swiveling his stool and standing. "If anything looks questionable we'll call for reinforcements."

Rove looked questioningly at Roam. "Maybe Rune would be better, he can detect danger faster. That's if Kya and her minions don't fly under his radar again."

"I'll be fine here with your parents and Teagan, Cowboy," Shayne said, fluttering her eyelashes and smiling up at him. "Go with your brothers. I'll be safe here until you return."

Rune crammed three pretzels into his mouth before he could laugh out loud. His big brother was done for, and all it had taken was for Kya to show up and threaten Shayne's existence. He grabbed Teagan's hand and spun her around. "I'll be back soon," he said once his mouth was empty and could give her a quick kiss. He turned to Rove. "Better give your girl a kiss since we'll be gone for a few. I don't want you missing her too much."

"Shut up, Rune," Rove answered, shoving him in the shoulder and laughing. "Let's go."

Rune laughed, grabbing a handful of pretzels and handing the bag off to Shayne. "He's saving up for later. Be prepared!" he said, and ran out the back door.

18

He had known it was here, somewhere within these castle walls. Finding it had taken Riebl the entire time they had been here. This wasn't the first castle Riebl had ever been in, although it was the most spectacular in arrangement and décor, if Riebl cared about any of that. He knew the armory had to be somewhere on the first floor. Most castles harbored their weapons within the Great Hall itself, but not Merlin, he had tucked it away to appear hidden. Riebl had literally stumbled into the room adjacent to the Great Hall, behind a hidden door in one of the panels, and now he couldn't take his eyes off the weaponry.

Racks had been built into the walls to hold swords of varying lengths and widths, daggers, knives, armor, helmets and everything else one searching for the ultimate weapon and protection would find. Riebl could've drooled, that is, if he hadn't been interrupted.

A movement out of the corner of his eye had him turning as darkness traveled, slithering across the dark and light gray tiles. Riebl took several hurried steps backward as the blackness grew in size consuming the area quickly. He banked to the right, grabbing a random sword out of the rack and slashing it from side to side, but still the blackness traveled backing him up into the wall of swords.

The blackness had substance to it, not like before where it traveled like fog, clinging to his clothing. Now it grabbed at him with force, clamping onto his leg making him yell out and shake it as he tried to get free. Fear overtook his senses as the blackness began to grow in front of him, taking on the shape of a person. It stood in front of him unmoving while laughter boomed out across the room.

Kya's full and deep laughter had her bending at the waist as it consumed her. "If only you could see your face!" She finally bellowed out.

Riebl swallowed, afraid to move, as the black figure stood stock still in front of him. Its body looked human-like with the absence of any parts that would distinguish between male or female. Its face was as black as the rest of it, no eye sockets, no nostrils, no lips. Just a complete mass of blackness.

"What's the matter, Riebl? Creepy black mutant got your tongue?" She howled in laughter, slapping her thigh and wiping at her eyes. "I'd say that was a complete success, exactly the reaction I was hoping for." She stepped up behind the black figure, flicking her wrist. The black mass dissolved to join the blackness still floating above the floor.

"What...what was that...that thing?" Riebl asked, unable to control his trembling voice.

Kya smiled, her eyes shining with complete happiness at her accomplishment. "He was just one of my army."

"Your...your army?"

"Yes," Kya answered, running her hands down her new, red velvet dress with blackness reaching out from under its long skirt. "A spell, in that fabulous book I found! I just got the final ingredient and was able to complete it!" She clapped her hands excitedly. "I can't wait to use my army against those despicable Gustavos." She turned excited eyes at Riebl just seconds before she touched his arm. "Let's try it out now, shall we?"

How strange, this book of the Gustavo's, Teagan thought as she carried it out the back door to the deck and sat in one of the chairs at the table. She placed her feet on one of the table rungs and held the book on her thighs. She ran one hand down the blank cover, wondering what it meant to have a book with no name. What kind of author would leave the cover of their book blank? Isn't that what most people looked to first, the cover? She carefully lifted the large book, feeling its weight in her hands, and turned it to look at its spine. Here too, it was blank. Why?

"What is it, girl?"

"Geez!" Teagan jumped, holding the book to her chest hoping to calm her beating heart. "I didn't know you were behind me."

Shayne grabbed a chair, sliding it back to move it closer to Teagan. "Sorry. But you had your eyes all scrunched up and my mama always says to not do that or you'll have permanent wrinkles there, and those you don't want because when you get old you'll have a permanent scowl on your face."

Teagan raised her eyebrows at her best friend, remembering just how eccentric Shayne's mama could sometimes be.

"Don't look at me that way," Shayne said, placing her own feet next to Teagan's and crossing her ankles. "I'm not the one who looked like they were trying to decide if they swallowed an orange or a lemon."

Teagan laughed. "Now you're sounding just like your mama."

"Thank you." Shayne smiled. "Now tell me why you're risking a future with wrinkles by worrying about something with that book."

"Why do you think it's about this book?" Teagan asked, placing the book back on her thighs.

"Because you were staring at it like you are some kind of librarian. Spill girl, I don't have all night. Well, maybe I do, but then the saying would be obsolete. So spill."

Teagan looked sheepishly at her friend. "Every time I look at Roam and Maya together these words keep invading my mind."

Shayne smiled, shaking her head slightly. "Don't look at me like you're going crazy, because you're not." Shayne touched Teagan on the shoulder. "What are the words that keep replaying in your head?"

"Light and dark."

Shayne scrunched her own eyes staring at the book. It took all of Teagan's willpower not to mention wrinkles. "Why?"

"I don't know," Teagan answered, shrugging. "But I think it has something to do with this book."

"Has it happened before? The words I mean. Did they pop into your head before when you looked at this book?"

Teagan thought for a moment, shaking her head. "No. Although I'm pretty sure it's happened whenever Roam and Maya were near it."

"Then open it."

Teagan grasped the book's cover with her fingers just as clapping began.

"Oh, look! How wonderful, two of the sisters!"

The deck table upturned when Teagan jumped up, her fangs descending and the book falling open on the deck at her feet.

Kya's eyes looked to the book then back at Teagan, a smile slowly creeping across her lips. "Would that be my book?" Kya asked, pointing with one long fingernail.

With only a thought Teagan's sword appeared in her left hand while she slid the book with the heel of her shoe closer to her friend. Teagan watched Kya's movements carefully as the sorceress stared back at her, a coy smile on her lips. Blackness traveled out from underneath her red velvet dress to float above the ground and climb the nearest trees to spread out and block the sunlight. When Teagan saw movement behind Kya, she darted her eyes quickly over the sorceress' shoulder to see Riebl standing two feet behind her, partially hidden by one of the trees.

"Send a message to Rune," Teagan sent silently to Shayne.

"Already done," Shayne answered. *"What are we going to do in the meantime?"*

"You'll be doing nothing but staying behind me," Teagan answered, her eyes never leaving Kya's. The sorceress stood in the yard, her dress swaying as more blackness seeped out from underneath to climb the side of the deck where it stopped, as if waiting to be told what to do next.

"I was hoping for more of an audience," Kya said, smiling. "Where is your other sister?"

"I don't have any sisters," Teagan countered, her sword humming in her hands wanting to fight. "I think you're becoming confused in your obsession with the brothers who live here."

Kya laughed. "I can't believe how none of you seem to know what has been written." She shook her head as she raised her arms in front of her body, palms facing up. "I guess you'll have to play with my new friend alone."

Blackness swirled in front of the deck, taking on the form of a mini tornado. The wind howled as it spun, sending out black flashes of lightning.

"Get inside, Shayne!" Teagan yelled, as the mini tornado thundered, the deck chairs flying off the deck and into the woods.

"I can't!" Shayne yelled back, her voice muffled. "I can't open the door, it's stuck!"

Teagan backed up, grabbing onto the door herself with her free hand. She yanked, but it was held fast. She looked up into the glass in the door, Adrianna stood with Excalibur motioning for her and Shayne to move out of the way with Dimitri behind her. Teagan locked eyes with Rune's dad, who nodded and pointed toward the yard. She knew she had to fight alone, at least for now.

Teagan grabbed Shayne, shoving her down behind the upturned deck table. "Please protect her," she whispered, shoving the table and Shayne, closer to the wall of the house. *"Whatever you do, don't let go of that book!"*

"Not planning to," Shayne replied. *"This probably isn't the time to tell you this, but I'm terrified."*

"Me too, Shay," Teagan answered. For the first time since bonding with the sword, she was afraid. *"Where are the boys and Maya?"*

"Kya put a barrier over the house. Rove is trying to break through but is saying Kya must have strengthened it. It won't give easily."

Teagan took a deep breath, rolling and relaxing her shoulders. Even with the sword begging to fight and making her body shiver with anticipation, she was still afraid. She was alone to fight whatever Kya was sending. She watched as the blackness continued to swirl as it began to lift off the ground, two black feet appearing followed by connected legs. *"We're about to have company!"* she yelled in her mind, as Shayne yelped in fear.

"OMG! What is that, Teagan? What are we going to do?"

"I'm going to fight," Teagan answered out loud, lifting her chin and staring out at Kya and the now fully formed blackness. As the body of blackness took a step forward, Teagan clasped the sword with both hands, dividing it into two. She fully allowed the swords power into her mind.

The power was outstanding! Fear vanished to be replaced by every move she could make with these swords. Teagan planted her feet to be equal with her shoulders, her left slightly forward. She raised her arms, her left arm on top and her right directly underneath it as if she were going to make an X with the swords. She took in a breath, relaxing her muscles and feeling the calmness and the knowledge the swords provided as she watched and waited, completely ready. When the black figure walked through the floating blackness across the ground, the blackness at its feet began shooting toward her. She slashed at it and watched as it broke apart. When another shot in her direction she parried, easily slicing it. Teagan smiled as the black figure stepped onto the deck and continued to walk toward her. She could feel her body relaxing to prepare for what she already knew she was going to do. As soon as it was within range, Teagan spun, both blades cutting the body completely in half. It crumpled to the deck, slithering back towards its master.

Kya sneered, her eyes shining. Teagan watched and waited for what this sorceress would do next. She wasn't prepared when strong arms seized her from behind and began squeezing. Teagan looked down only to see blackness. Somehow, one of the black beings had developed behind her without her knowledge. No matter what she did, she couldn't break free from its grasp.

"Such a pity," Kya said, walking towards the deck. "How sad that the other two will never know you three are sisters. Without you, they will never be able to stop me or my army."

"You're lying!" Teagan shouted, shuddering when her swords spoke to her.

"Am I?" Kya answered, hitching her dress to step onto the deck. "You can't tell me you haven't felt some kind of connection to the other two." Kya stopped in front of her, placing a long fingernail on her chin as if in deep thought. "Of course, you could always submit to me and you will live."

Teagan smiled, feeling the cold steel of her blades next to her sides just as a purple sheen exploded sending debris of rocks and dirt to fly in their direction. "Never," she answered as she drove the blades home. She ignored the feel of her own flesh cutting as the tips of the blades found their mark and drove into its blackness, just as something large and white took Kya right off her feet. Kya flew backward off the deck, reaching an arm down as she flew to grab onto Riebl and vanish from sight.

19

"TEAGAN!" RUNE HAD SEEN WHAT SHE HAD DONE, TAKING OUT WHATEVER that black figure had been behind her, and cutting herself in the process. "Oh, please, no!" he yelled, jumping and clearing the edge of the deck to land inches from her as blood pooled and soaked into her shirt. He reached out to grab her and froze.

A silvery, whiteness traveled up Teagan's arms beginning at the swords still in her grasp. As soon as it reached her sides, it became brighter, enveloping her body. Fear stabbed at his heart as Teagan looked at him with an expression that must duplicate his own.

He reached out a hand that was shaking to latch onto her arm coated with whiteness. The whiteness traveled onto his own hand sending a tingling sensation and a gentle wave of calmness throughout his body. He watched in awe, the whiteness becoming more intense at her sides, the redness fading. Relief poured into Rune as he looked into her eyes and gasped out the breath he had been holding.

"Your sword is healing you." He smiled, letting more tears run freely down his face. He watched as Teagan looked down in disbelief, lifting one arm and then the other. Her eyes shot to his and she smiled, her swords disappearing just seconds before she dove into his arms.

"I thought I was a goner," she whispered, snuggling in as close as she could get. "I didn't even think of what would happen until after, and I couldn't think of anything but losing you forever."

Rune placed his chin on the top of her head and held on tight. "I don't know what I would've done if I'd lost you."

"Let's make a deal to never find out."

Rune nodded, watching as Rove stood in the center of the deck scanning the area around them, their dad's hand on his shoulder. He lifted concerned eyes at his younger brother.

"Where's Shayne?" he asked.

"I'm here!" came a muffled reply. "Is that thing gone? Did you get it, Rove?"

"Shayne?" Rove grabbed hold of the table yanking it away from the wall, letting it roll towards Roam. Shayne slowly lifted her head from her upturned knees, relief showing on an otherwise frightened face.

"Oh, thank goodness!" she said as Rove reached down and pulled her into his arms, their large book clunking open onto the deck. "That thing was the worst thing I've ever seen, even creepier than in my vision."

"I'm so sorry," Rove said into her hair holding her tightly. "I shouldn't have left. Kya had a barrier in place and we couldn't get through as easily as before. I could hear you in my mind, how afraid you were."

"It's not your fault," Shayne answered. "I told you to go."

"So, Shayne's vision came true?" Maya asked, helping Roam to upright the table.

"No," came Shayne's muffled reply, her face buried into Rove's chest. "Her dress was red, not black."

"Why do I get the feeling that whatever Shayne saw in her vision is going to be far worse than what we have dealt with so far?" Roam said, bending down to grab their book from off the deck.

"No, Roam. Wait!" Teagan pushed away from Rune staring down at the book. It was lying open to a page Rune hadn't seen before. It was beautiful, with colors so rich and so vibrant, of lush green meadows and sturdy green leaved trees. Fairies, hundreds of them, hid amongst their branches.

"What is it, Finn?" Rove asked over Shayne's head.

"The book talking to you again?" Shayne asked, turning her head to look at her.

"Our book talks to you?" Rune asked, lifting his eyebrows in question.

Teagan went down on her haunches in front of the book. "Sort of. I mean, every time I look at Roam and Maya together, particularly when this book is around, the words light and dark echo in my mind. At first I thought it was because of what Kya said and our needing to find a book of light and dark. But now I was wondering if it didn't have to do with this book. So, I brought the book out here to see if something would jump out at me. I think this might be it."

"That page wasn't there before," Maya said as she knelt down next to her.

Teagan turned the page. "Neither was this one." Complete blackness, so dark as if it were nonexistent, covered the entire page.

"Is the book still talking to you?" Shayne asked.

"Actually, it is." She flipped between the two pages. "Light and dark."

"What's the significance of these pages?" Maya asked. "Why were they added and by whom?"

"Maybe we should take the book inside and look at it together," Mom suggested.

Teagan shook her head, flipping back to the page of beauty "There's something hidden here, underneath this page."

Rune couldn't move fast enough, Teagan raised her left hand with the Celtic tattoo and ran her fingers down the page. All Rune could do was watch in amazement when each fairy lifted from their hiding place to join in the center of the page. With a wink and wave, the fairies moved as one, each taking a piece of beauty and pulling it backward to form a border around a blank canvas underneath. Words began to flow across the emptiness, dancing across the page in elegant cursive from an invisible, artistic hand.

Teagan picked up the book, cradling it in her arms. Rune placed his arm protectively across her shoulders as everyone else gathered around and Teagan began to read. "'The Enchanted Realm is closed to all non-magical beings. It remains magically locked to keep the mortal world and the enchanted one separate, to live separate lives on separate realms. Once every one-thousand years, a key and rune become available in the mortal world to one magical being. The rune is the only object which can turn the key to open the gateway between Mt. Ciadar and the Enchanted Realm on a day without a night during the summer solstice.'"

"It's you," Teagan said quietly into the silence, looking up at him. "You're the rune."

"And this is the key," Rune added, pulling his chain from under his shirt to expose his necklace with the added key.

"I think Teagan just found the book of Light and Dark," Roam stated.

"And where to find the Enchanted Realm," Mom said, looking with concern at Dad.

"And we have the key." Rune lifted the chain. "Although this is the oddest key I've ever seen."

"We now know when a day without a night is," Maya said. "The summer solstice."

"When is the summer solstice?" Rove asked.

"June 21st," Shayne answered.

"Is there anything you don't know?" Rove asked, looking down at her.

Shayne shrugged. "I have my hobbies."

"And speaking Latin?"

"It's more being able to read Latin, than speaking it," Shayne answered.

"Is that why Rune's key is written in Latin instead of English? So only the one who is meant to have it is able to read it?" Teagan asked.

"But I can't read Latin," Rune interjected. "Is this key meant for Shayne?"

"No, I don't think so," Mom said, putting her hand on her youngest son's shoulder. "It makes sense that you are the rune. Why else would I have named you Rune?"

"Because Pappy told you too," Rune answered smugly.

"If Pappy knew all of this was going to happen," Rove asked angrily. "Why didn't he just tell us as soon as we got our powers so we were prepared?"

"Maybe he couldn't," Teagan answered.

"Or maybe he didn't know," Maya corrected. "This book he knows about," she said, touching it "We've all looked through these pages countless times. These pages weren't here before. Teagan was meant to find this page about the Enchanted Realm." Maya scratched her head. "I have to admit I am confused though."

"About?" Rune asked.

"Well, why the black page?" Maya flipped to it. "I understand each page has a front and a back, and this one to signify the dark for the light. Why isn't it a picture in black? Why does it look like a black hole?"

"What if Finn touches it?"

"Rove!" Rune stated forcefully.

Rove pointed down at the page. "Finn touched the light page and we get another prophecy. So far, I haven't seen her touch the dark page. I'm just wondering if something will happen if she touches it."

"You want another prophecy?" Roam questioned.

"Of course not!" Rove snapped back. "There was a reason for the one page. What is the reason for this one?"

"What if she gets sucked into the book?" Rune argued. "How do we get her back?"

"Do you feel a threat?" Rove questioned, crossing his arms across his chest.

"No," Rune answered, crossing his own. "But lately that doesn't seem to mean anything!"

"How about you, Finn?" Rove asked turning toward her. "Do you feel anything? Any threats? Any harm to be done to you? Your sword wanting to come out and play?"

"What is wrong with you, Rove?" Rune demanded, taking a step in his brother's direction only for their dad to step between them.

"This arguing is getting us nowhere," Dad said placing a hand on each of their chests and giving them a push backward. "Let Teagan answer Rove's question, Rune." Dad raised a hand for quiet when Rune began to protest. "Rove's question is acceptable. Teagan, What do you think?"

"I think..." she looked at Rove, then to Rune, "...my sword isn't saying anything which tells me there's no threat here, at least not to me. I don't even feel the pull anymore." She looked down at the page in question. "I feel... nothing," she stated as she plopped her hand onto the page.

Rune jumped toward her but a purple barrier got to Teagan first, blocking her body from the page. Rune looked to Maya, silently thanking her.

"It's all good," Teagan said, lifting her eyes to theirs. "It's just a page." She proved it by running her hand over it and lifting her hand to touch it over and over.

"You're sure?" Rune asked.

"I'm sure," she said and nodded. "Go ahead, touch the page and see for yourself."

Rune waited for the barrier to drop and reached over to touch the page himself. He sighed, relief and anger filling him. "Please, Teagan. Don't do that again."

"I'm sorry. But I knew you wouldn't let me and we needed to know."

"And what if something had happened, Teagan? What then, huh?" He backed up, not really sure what he was doing as Teagan looked at him with pleading eyes. With a thought he transported to the cave where it had all began. He needed time to think and to be alone.

"She destroyed him!"

Kya slammed her hands down onto the center island in the kitchen, open books toppling off its edges to slam to the floor. Riebl leaned up against the wall, pressing his hand on his arm to stop the bleeding Kya's nails had caused.

"It isn't possible!" she snarled, taking her arm and clearing the rest of the island. "My army is supposed to be indestructible! How is it that the sword wielding fiend was able to destroy him by herself?"

"Maybe because she's good and you're bad?"

Kya's head slowly turned in his direction. "What makes you think I'm talking to you?"

Riebl looked around the kitchen. "I seem to be the only person here, so who else would you be talking to, Kya? The walls, the floor, your missing army man?" He stepped away from the wall, pointing a finger in her direction as his anger built. "You brought me into this, into your employ. What else would you like me to do but to be quiet? I'm tired of being your personal punching bag. The one to whom you always throw insults. You asked me to come with you. You asked me to help you fight the Gustavos and you treat me as if I wasn't even here!"

Kya straightened, a sneer appearing. "That's right," she stated. "You're not even here."

Riebl's eyes grew wide as Kya brought up her hand, "Wait!" he yelled, thankful when Kya's hand stilled. "The wizard is starting to trust me," he said, trying to calm his nerves as Kya continued to stare at him, her hand still in the air. "I went to him, trying to turn him to work for us. I don't think I can completely turn him, but I might be able to convince him to do something, anything, which may help us."

"You went to the wizard, behind my back!" Kya yelled, her face turning a darker shade of red than before. "How do I know you're not trying to turn the wizard against me?"

Riebl stood firm, hoping she wouldn't notice his fear as he tried to come up with anything to save his own skin. "I thought I would try, to help us both. I can't do it on my own, but with your help I might be able to...to get him to tell me where the doorway is to the Enchanted Realm."

Kya smiled, closing her hand and nodding. "Yes, that might work. You could go to the wizard and if he tells you where the gateway is, I will spare your miserable life."

Riebl took in a shuddering breath as Kya turned away from him. He at least had bought himself a little more time.

"Pick up that mess," she ordered, walking to the doorway leading to the dungeon. "I need to devise a plan to get that book from those brats!" She spun around and smiled as she waved a hand at him.

Riebl dropped to the floor, his head between his hands as a pain like nothing he had ever felt before slashed at the inside of his skull. "Now I will be able to hear anything you say to that wizard," Riebl heard her say as tears and sweat traveled down his face and hands. "I must protect myself, after all."

Riebl slowly lifted his head as the pain subsided. The doorway where Kya had been was now empty and he wondered if he had just made matters worse. He let his arms slide down to the floor. He was going to have to come up with something to convince Merlin to help him get rid of Kya, without her knowing what he was doing.

20

"You're going to barbeque, after all that happened today?" Rove asked, leaning back against the counter as steaks were removed from the freezer to be placed under water running in the kitchen sink.

"Sure, why not?" Dimitri answered, removing the last steak from its packaging. "Life continues on even after visits from psycho freak sorceresses, and the unveiling of a prophecy."

"Speaking of Rune, when do you think he'll be back?" Rove asked. "He's been gone for two hours now." He snatched a chip as it fell into the plastic bowl Roam was pouring them into.

"He just needed some time alone," Adrianna answered while sprinkling seasoning onto the steaks. "He'll be home soon."

Teagan plopped down onto a kitchen stool next to Shayne, placing her face between fisted hands.

"Stop pouting," Shayne said, inside her head.

"Easy for you to say," Teagan answered, lowering her head more when the boys and Maya looked discreetly her way knowing they heard Shayne's telepathic message. *"Your boyfriend didn't leave because of something you did."*

"It wasn't all because of what you did."

Teagan lifted her head, and tilted it towards Shayne.

"It wasn't me," Shayne said, pointing at her chest.

"It was me."

Rune appeared with a daisy in his grasp. "It was stupid of me to leave." He looked Teagan in the eye, extending the flower closer to her. *"I wanted to protect you. Not for you to protect yourself."*

"Such a guy thing," Shayne interjected, shaking her head. "You always have to be the knight in shining armor." She jumped in her chair when Teagan kicked her under the table. "Ouch, what did you do that for?"

"Shush," Teagan answered, her eyes riveted on Rune while a smile played across her lips. "You just spoke to me telepathically."

Rune smiled. "Kind of like Maya. I was able to hear you after you found the prophecy in our book whenever you spoke with Shayne."

"I can speak with you now?" Teagan stood. Nothing could make her happier than being able to converse with him telepathically.

"And everyone else apparently."

Teagan laughed, taking the daisy from Rune and turning toward Rove. "That's one of my major downfalls. I often forget to put up a block. Might as well get used to it."

"So, no different from Shayne then?" Rove winked as the back door swung open and Vlad stepped inside, his face a glowing red. Laughter escaped Rove's lips making Teagan stifle her own.

"Didn't I warn you to wear the sunscreen I gave you?" Rove said, still laughing.

"Not now," Vlad replied, pulling his t-shirt away from his skin in discomfort and revealing just how sunburned he was. "We have more pressing matters."

"How can a nightwalker get sunburned?" Shayne asked in disbelief. "I mean, you're supposed to just go poof in the sun. Why would you abuse a special gift from a Sorceress to get a sunburn?"

Vlad actually rolled his eyes before going back to the screen door and pulling Diego inside. "Like I said, we have more pressing matters than my unwanted sunburn. Where's Teagan?"

"I'm right here," she answered, feeling uneasy as she looked at Diego standing uncomfortably in the kitchen. "What's wrong? Where's Posh?"

Vlad ran a hand through his long, black hair. "That's why Diego is here," he answered, as the back door opened again and Radek, Aradney and Francesca stepped inside.

Fear bubbled to the surface as Teagan stared at them all, Diego would never be here without Posh. She carefully set the daisy down on the counter trying to control her emotions. "Where's Posh?" she asked again, fear lacing her words.

Diego lifted his head. "She left," he answered, holding out a piece of paper in his grasp.

Teagan couldn't move. It had to be some kind of mistake! Posh would never leave without talking to her first, and she would never leave Diego unprotected. Rune pulled her close as Shayne walked to Diego and took the paper from his fingers. She scanned the message looking up at Vlad in puzzlement.

"I don't understand," Shayne said. "What does this mean?"

Vlad took the paper from Shayne and stepped in front of Teagan, placing his fingers under her chin and wiping away a tear. He held the paper up and began to read. "'To my amazing friends. By the time you read this, I will be gone. Please don't search for me. I have the sickness and don't want you to see me as my mind leaves me to leave behind an empty shell." Vlad's voice hitched, he wiped away tears of his own before continuing on. "'Please give Diego a home, and make him feel wanted. He has come a long way since leaving the rogue vampires, and since he was spared, I think he is deserving of all of your friendships. Please tell Teagan how much I love her and I will miss her until the day I am gone. I will watch the sunrise and think of her each and every day. With light and love, Posh.'"

Tears left Teagan's body in a rush, making her gasp as sobbing overtook her body. Rune's arms came around her, drawing her in close to whisper softly in her ear and rock her gently.

"I am so sorry," Vlad cried, reaching out and running a hand down her hair.

Her anger flared. Teagan shoved Rune away as she turned to face Vlad. She thought of her swords just seconds before they appeared one in each hand. She took a step towards Vlad, tears streaming down her face. "It's your fault!" she yelled, her body shaking and her chest heaving in sorrow. "If you wouldn't have sent her inside she never would've came down with the sickness!"

"I know," Vlad pleaded, shaking his head at someone behind her as she advanced and Vlad backed up. "But Teagan, she knew what she might get herself into before she volunteered to go in. It tears me up inside with fear, I can't imagine what she must be going through."

Teagan stopped, she knew he was right. Posh had volunteered. She and Posh were the only ones who Godard hadn't known or recognized. Her arms dropped to her sides, her swords still pointing outward. "Why did she leave like this?" Teagan asked. "We could've tried to find a cure."

"There is no cure, Teagan. You know that," Vlad responded sympathetically.

"But we could've been there for her," Teagan answered as she looked down, tears falling onto the floor.

"She didn't want any of us to watch her suffer," Diego added.

Teagan looked up. Diego's face wet from the tears he shed for their friend. With a thought, Teagan allowed her swords to leave and pulled Diego into her embrace. He sobbed, gut wrenching sobs.

"She saved me from them," Diego said, his words muffled by Teagan's shoulder.

"I know," Teagan answered. "And I am grateful every day she did."

"This sickness," Teagan heard Shayne ask. "Does it make the whites of the eyes turn red?"

Teagan lifted her head as she heard Radek respond. "Yes. It seems to be the only known visible characteristic. Why do you ask, Shayne?"

"Because Posh isn't the only one who's sick."

"Who else?" Teagan asked alarmed, darting her eyes first at Rune, then his brothers. "Who else, Shayne?"

"Riebl," Shayne answered. "He was in the vision I saw with Kya wearing the black dress. The whites of his eyes are red when they come."

THE WALLS WERE CRAWLING with bugs. Riebl stood in the middle of the kitchen and stared. How was he going to get down to the dungeon now?

Where had they come from? He ran both hands through his hair, turning this way and that as more bugs came to crawl on the floor by his feet. He stamped his boots trying to smash the pests, but it was useless. More and more bugs crawled covering the entire space of the floor.

"What are you doing?" Kya sauntered into the room, her long dress swaying as her bare feet walked over the bug-filled floor.

How could she do that, walking over them like that? Riebl stared at her feet until they stopped in front of him.

"Why are you just standing there like that?"

Riebl tore his eyes away from the army of crawling bugs to look at Kya. "Bugs...your walking on bugs..."

"So you've found the liquor cabinet? Just look at you, all sweaty with blood shot eyes? There aren't any bugs in here you drunken fool. Get out of my way," she said shoving him backward. "I have work to do."

Riebl's back slammed into the wall. He quickly jumped forward slapping and running his hands down his back as the bugs whined under his feet.

"Stop that hideous noise!" Kya demanded, scowling at him. "Go find somewhere else to hang your drunken head." She grabbed a bunch of books from off the center island, some falling to the floor again. "Worthless, that's what you are," she said, picking up a smaller book and making her way back to the stairs leading to the dungeon.

Riebl stared after her, running a shaking hand down his face. He wasn't drunk. Even if he could he wouldn't, alcohol messed with a vampire's senses. Riebl wanted to correct her, to remind her he could only ingest blood, why else would the refrigerator have blood bags in it? He darted his eyes around the now bug-less room. Not even one carcass lay where Kya had stepped. Was he going mad? He shakily took a step and stopped dead in his tracks when her words registered in his confused brain.

Riebl stumbled, righting himself and hurrying to the bathroom near the stairs leading to the dungeon, slapping on the light. Slowly he stepped up to the mirror above the sink and lifted his eyes to look at his reflection. Red, the whites of his eyes were tainted red.

"No, no, no!" he panicked, turning on the water and slapping it onto his face and eyes. But when he looked again, it was still there. He had the sickness, he was going to lose his mind as Gabriel had and he was going to die. Rage replaced his fear as he cried out and slammed his fists into the mirror. He paid no mind as it shattered and dug into his fisted hands, his blood dripping to land into the sink.

"Merlin will fix me," he snarled. "I'll release him and he'll have no other choice but to fix me, or I will bring his family here and he can watch them all die."

21

HE COULDN'T GET COMFORTABLE. HE HAD WOKEN IN A SWEAT AN HOUR AGO, tossing and turning. It wasn't how much steak or potatoes he ate, or even the pie. His bed seemed uncomfortable, his room too hot, and his mind too busy. Even with a gentle breeze blowing in through his open window, he still felt clammy and closed in. Agitated, he flipped over and glanced at his digital clock's glowing face, 1:17 a.m. It was no use, sleep wasn't returning anytime soon.

Rove placed a barrier up in his mind and threw off his covers to sit on the edge of his bed, no reason to wake his brothers with his sleeplessness. He scrubbed his tired eyes and ran his fingers through his messed up hair. As he brought his head up, a movement caught his attention out of the corner of his eye. Slowly, Rove placed his feet on the floor and summoned one of his ropes into his right hand. With one quick precise move, Rove was standing and facing an image of himself in his bedroom mirror fastened to the inside of his open closet door. With his heart beating in overtime, Rove laughed at himself and willed his rope away.

"I really need to get some sleep." He turned, and froze. There had definitely been a movement and he had a good feeling it had to do with his bedroom mirror.

Slowly, he lowered his hand and within seconds, his rope rematerialized.

He turned toward his mirror only to be greeted, once again, with his own reflection. It stared back at him showing what others saw each and every day, attitude. But something wasn't right. Carefully, he took a step forward, summoning his second rope reminding himself to not set it to flame. The last thing he needed was to set the carpet on fire. He took another step and tilted his head in confusion. When did his hair get longer? His mind wandered unexpectedly, bringing an image of Vlad into his mind's eye and how the centuries old vampire had long, black hair. The mirror wavered, like water when a hand runs across its surface, bringing forth an image of Vlad holding his ropes.

Rove stumbled back, his eyes wide, staring back at a mimicking Vlad. Rove raised his right arm, getting ready to flick his weapon up like a lasso at the mirror and watched as Vlad's reflection did the same. With thoughts of removing the barrier in his mind, Rove thought of his brothers. The mirror wavered again showing his own reflection with his hair shifting between white and blue streaks, instead of his normal red.

The reflection in the mirror's chest heaved as Rove's eyes remained on his changing features. He knew he was awake, he knew he was himself, maybe it was the mirror itself. With extreme caution, Rove willed one of his ropes away. He watched as a presently reflected Roam did the same. He brought his left arm up so his rope was closer to the mirror, and reached out with his right. His reach was tentative until he finally touched the glass and was greeted with a smooth, cool surface.

A heavy sigh left his lips as his hand remained on the mirror. "It's not a portal," he said with relief, running his fingertips up and down the mirror just to make sure. Then it had to be enchanted. He stared into the eyes of Rune as the thought bounced around in his mind. Pappy could do that. Maybe he had found a way to contact them after all. Unfortunately, it didn't seem to be a two-way mirror and Rove had no idea on how to respond back.

"Well, Pappy," Rove said into the mirror. "If it is you, it'll have to wait until morning. Maya and Shayne would know how to work this thing." He smiled at the thought of Shayne, willing his remaining rope away and stepping from the mirror. What he did need right now was some air.

It was dark as he floated down next to the side of the house, the stars shining brightly in the midnight sky. It was amazing how the stars could give enough light so he could look out into the woods that surrounded their house. So much had happened just inside these woods, things that he never thought possible, and some things, which he wasn't exactly proud. He breathed in deeply, welcoming the breeze that suddenly picked up, and turned slowly toward the backyard when laughter joined in with it.

The tree house was lit brightly, beams of light reaching down to the ground through the vacant space where the wall used to be. How he had missed it, he had no idea. Shayne and Teagan, dressed in matching shorts and tank top pajamas, sat across from each other at the square picnic table. Their hands flying as they each slapped cards onto the table, in what must've been, the fastest game of Speed Rove had ever seen. Shayne suddenly shot up, her arms raised above her head, as she did a silent victory dance. Then laughed heartily when Teagan picked up one of the piles, and expertly shot the cards out of her fingers to hit Shayne square in the chest. Rove leaned against the wall of the house, in the shadows, to watch.

It was interesting to watch them with their guards down, acting like two average teenagers. They picked up the cards, shuffled them, and dealt them out to start another fast-paced game. All the while, laughing at each other freely and easily as if they didn't have a care in the world.

"Quit cheating, Teags!" Shayne said laughing as cards fell to the floor.

"You should talk, Shay! You're the one cheating! You just put a two on a six."

"Did not you liar!" Shayne laughed slapping down another card, only for Teagan to pick it up and throw it back at her.

Rove quietly laughed right along with them, enjoying hearing their nicknames for each other and wondered why they never said them around anyone else. He was just thinking of waking his brothers when a wave of nausea hit him. He leaned heavily against the wall, his body breaking out in a cold sweat making him shiver. Images shot through his mind, too fast for him to keep up, of people he knew making him dizzy. Pain tore into his mind making him cry out. He fell to his knees on the ground, his forehead touching the cool earth, his hands on the sides of his head. He felt two sets of warm hands on his back as he rocked in pain.

"Who is it?" he heard Shayne ask.

"One of the boys," Teagan answered.

"I knew that," Shayne retorted. "I was asking which one."

"I'm trying to find out but I can't see the streaks in his hair."

Rove shook, he felt frozen even in the warm June night. How could he feel so cold when it had to be nearly seventy degrees?

"Maybe we should get Adrianna?"

"Don't you dare!" he snarled, lifting his head.

"Rove? OMG! Let us help you!"

"No, Shay. Look, white streaks. It's Rune."

"Ah, his streaks just changed to blue, Teags."

"Back up, Shay."

He was really changing? It hadn't been the mirror after all? Two hands grabbed him, dragging him to his feet. At first, he thought one of his brothers had come out, until he was slammed against the side of the house and a sword was at his throat.

"Who are you?"

Man she was strong when she wielded her sword. "I'm Rove...oh man...please let me go..."

"Teagan, it is Rove."

Teagan shook her head, her grip strengthening. "No, he's not. Look, Shay, his hair keeps changing color. He's got to be Riebl with a spell gone wrong."

Panic tore into Rove as Teagan's face took on its warrior mode. She was going to kill him and there was nothing he was going to be able to do about it. He felt the sword slice his skin and Shayne's image came into his mind.

"O...M...G...," Shayne said slowly as she backed up even more. "He just turned into me!"

Crap, he hadn't meant to do that. This wasn't going to help in his favor at all. Rove concentrated, hoping he turned back into himself. Teagan's grip tightened more making him cough as his air supply slowly began to be cut off. Man his throat was burning.

"Last chance, pal," Teagan warned. Her grip lessened by his throat, but still strong as he was held tight against the wall. "Who are you and what do you want?"

"Finn...it's me..." Rove rasped out. "I swear...Finn...it's me..."

Teagan stared at him, cocking her head to the side, "Don't play games with me!"

"Teagan, listen to me," Shayne pleaded touching her on the shoulder. "He called you Finn. Only Rove calls you Finn. Riebl wouldn't know that!"

Her grip lessened more, her eyes staring him down.

"It's me, Finn. I swear it's me."

"What did Rove do to one of his grandfathers the first time he saw me?"

Rove struggled to get his thoughts in order, he had to get this right or he was dead. A smile played across his lips as he remembered. "Which one? When I flipped Dracula, or when I almost set him on fire?"

He slid down the side of the house as Teagan let him go, coughing when his air supply returned full force. He slumped against the wall, his head pounding. Images kept coming and going as he tried desperately to get them under control and not throw up his dinner. He looked over just in time to see Teagan's head drop and her sword disappear.

"You were protecting Shayne," Rove rasped. "I wouldn't have expected anything less of you."

"But what if I hadn't listened and killed you?" Teagan asked, leaning against the house.

"You would've made sure I was Riebl before killing me. I'm sure of that."

"How can you be so sure?" she asked, looking at him.

Rove tried to clear his throat, but it remained raspy. "I'm confident you wouldn't take the chance of hurting Rune again. Your grip lessened so I could speak. Somewhere in your mind, you knew you had to be sure. Be confident that you can control yourself when you're wielding your sword."

She nodded, her eyes looking to the ground.

"You're one strong girl when you wield that sword of yours." Rove let his head fall back to rest on the wall. "Thanks for looking out for Shay." He was rewarded with the smile he had hoped for.

"Anytime. Sorry about your neck."

"It'll be gone by morning." Rove wiped off the already drying blood. "Just for the record, I probably would've beaten the snot out of you if the situation was reversed."

Teagan laughed. "You could've tried."

"So, how did you do it?" Shayne asked, handing him a half-full bottle of water while sitting down next to him.

"Do what?" he asked, taking a long pull from the bottle and letting the cool water soothe his throat.

"Boy, you really were oxygen deprived." She thumped her hand on his chest and looked up at him with her large gray eyes. "How did you change into Rune, then into me? Which, by the way, was creepy."

"I'm not really sure." Rove squished the now empty bottle with one hand, and placed his other on top of Shayne's. "I thought I saw a movement in my room. I initially thought Pappy was trying to contact me through my closet mirror. I had no idea it was actually me changing into different people."

"Probably what I would've assumed," Teagan responded. "Shay, you're the one with all the magic and witchcraft knowledge, you have to have some idea of what's happening to him."

"Actually, I might." She smiled. "You're yourself again. Are you doing that?"

"I think so. I have to keep an image of myself in my head but my mind keeps trying to change who I'm seeing."

"That's messed up." Teagan sat cross-legged on the ground. "What's your theory, Shay? Do you think Kya put a spell on him?"

Shayne shook her head. "You guys are part wizard, right?"

"That's what Pappy says."

"Rune can now teleport. So, I'm thinking that maybe your wizard powers are coming into play and I think you might be a shifter."

Rove cocked an eyebrow. "A shifter? That's a vampire trait. Vlad can turn into a bat."

"Vlad *can* turn into a bat," Shayne agreed. "But a shifter can turn into more than one thing."

"You're saying Vlad isn't a shifter?"

"No. He can turn into a bat because he's a vampire. You're turning into different people. Believe it or not, there's a difference."

The screen door whined open and Dad's darkened silhouette stood in its frame. "I was wondering who in the world was outside this early in the morning striking up a conversation," Dad said, his voice clipped and his hair standing on end. "Get to bed, all of you. Now."

Rove winced. "We're coming, Dad. Sorry we woke you."

"First you wake up your mother, now me. Don't expect to sleep all day, or pancakes for breakfast." The screen door slapped shut behind Dad as he continued to mumble threats on his way back to bed.

Rove stood, reaching a hand down to help Shayne to her feet. "Listen, I need to ask a favor."

Shayne brushed dirt off her pajama shorts. "What kind of favor?"

"Keeping this shifting thing between the three of us for now."

"Sure," Teagan answered shrugging. "We'll just let Adrianna slice and dice you when you change into your mom in front of her."

Rove ran a hand through his hair. "That's an image I really didn't want to have, but could very well come true. How about if I can keep it under control we keep it a secret?"

"Why don't you want to tell your brothers or Maya?" Shayne asked looking up at him, confused.

"I just have this feeling that it might come in handy when we least expect it."

"Least expect it," Teagan mimicked, nodding. "Good choice of words. That's exactly how your new power is working."

Shayne gave her a shove as they made their way to the back door. "If you feel it's important to keep this to ourselves for now, then we will. But if you change into someone unexpectedly, one of us is going to need to say something or you'll have a real-life flashback of how Teagan handled it."

Rove rubbed his healing neck. "Yeah, that's a flashback I don't want to relive again either." His thoughts wandered as he locked the back door and watched as the girls made their way down the basement stairs. Things could've gone much worse, and still could, if he didn't watch what he was doing.

22

SHE TWIRLED, CLAPPING HER HANDS LIKE A LITTLE GIRL PLAYING PRINCESS. THE dress was outstanding and it suited her perfectly. Kya ran her hands down its front as she stared at her reflection in the full-length mirror. No more of the medieval gowns that restricted her movements. This is what she had needed all along. The dress was as black as a starless night, with silver studs lining the V of the neckline. It fit snuggly down her body to whisper softly across her bare feet with a slit running from her thigh on her right side. She frowned for a moment, then snapped her fingers to coat her toenails with the same black as her razor sharp fingernails, and clapped with glee when she saw the effect. She twirled again, only stopping when she heard voices in her head and listened.

"If you know what's good for you," Riebl was saying. "You'll tell me where the entrance is to the Enchanted Realm."

"Why would I tell you that?" Merlin answered, in his stiff wizard tone. Kya could almost see him standing with his hands clasped in front of his body.

"Because if you do I'll find a way to release you."

Kya clucked her tongue in disagreement, slowly pacing in one of the massive bedrooms on the second floor.

"And if I don't?"

"Then I will bring your family here, one by one, and you will watch each and every one of them die."

Kya smiled, nodding slowly in agreement.

"You don't have that power," Merlin answered, fear lacing his words.

"I may not, but Kya does. All I need is to ask. She hates your family as much as I do!"

Kya heard the snarl in his voice, placing a hand over her heart in approval.

"Why do you have such hatred for my family? They don't know where the Enchanted Realm is, or how to get there. They have nothing to do with what you ask."

Kya waved her hand across the mirror's surface, she wanted to watch the fear displayed across his scraggily old face.

Riebl grabbed the bars and slammed his face between them looking wild and crazy. Kya had to contain herself from squealing with delight.

"Because your family demolished mine!" Riebl yelled, spittle flying to land on Merlin's face and torso. "Vladimir denied me to be a part of his family." Riebl pulled back, sneering at Merlin with absolute hatred. "Gabriel and Godard took me in and your grandsons destroyed them and everyone else! And what does Vlad and his clan get in exchange? The sun and food to eat! I have drank blood for more centuries than I can count and I deserve more!"

Merlin wiped at his face with the corner of his tattered sleeve. "I have nothing to do with what the Sorceress of the Sun granted Vlad and his followers with."

"That's why you're going to tell me where to find the Enchanted Realm," Riebl answered. "When the gateway is open I will be the one to tell the Sorceress where you are, and she will grant me the same as she granted Vlad."

Interesting, thought Kya as she watched Merlin for a reaction. She saw the smile poke at the wizard's lips. Stupid vampire.

"What makes you think you can get the gateway open even if I told you where it is?"

Riebl actually strutted as he paced. "Because Kya is building an army, an indestructible army. If you want to save your family, you'll tell me what I want to know."

Kya turned her fist in the air transporting Riebl to land at her feet. With a wave of her wrist he was slammed into the wall, and just to make her statement known, she slammed him a second time. Decorative paintings and ugly knickknacks hit the floor shattering.

"What're you doing!" he yelled, the drapery falling and covering him where he was sprawled out on the floor. He kicked at it, trying to disentangle himself. "I had him in the palm of my hand!"

"Who gave you permission to fill the wizard in on my army?" she asked in a quiet, controlled voice. She raised her hand and smiled as Riebl was lifted, his feet dangling underneath him and the drapery slithering to the floor.

"It just came out!" Riebl begged. "I didn't know it was a secret! I'm trying to turn the wizard to make him afraid!"

"Oh, you've made him afraid all right," Kya answered. "But you've also told him what I needed his blood for. If he finds his way out of his cell, he will know exactly how to stop us and my army. And that would be most unfortunate for you."

"For me?" Riebl was starting to sweat and Kya found that most appealing. "You mean for us!"

"No." Kya wagged a finger at him, causing the grip to tighten on his throat. She smiled happily when Riebl kicked his feet to get free. "You will pay the consequences. I will make sure of that."

She released him, smiling when he dropped to the floor and gasped for a breath. "You know," she said turning, her dress whispering against her legs. "I think it would be a good time to have you do a little favor for me."

Riebl scooted back on the floor, pressing his back into the wall.

"Aren't you going to ask me what kind of favor?" she challenged, smiling evilly. "That's okay, I'll just tell you." She twisted her wrist and Riebl lifted from the floor and was placed gently on his feet.

She began to pace, looking at him as she swung her arms. "I'm going to send you on a little field trip. I thought I'd send you alone, but what's the fun in that?"

"What...what kind of field trip?"

"He speaks!" Kya lifted her shoulders in excitement. "We're going to the Gustavo home and you're going to grab their book for me. Won't that be fun?"

RUNE JOGGED down the steps and practically danced into the kitchen, grabbing the first empty stool he could find and plopping down onto it. "Good morning everybody," he exclaimed, taking the offered cup of orange juice from his mom.

Teagan lifted her head and snarled at him as she pushed a soggy mess of Lucky Charms around in her bowl.

Rune lifted his eyebrows in question. "Didn't sleep well last night?"

"Try staying out until the wee hours of the morning," Dad answered, pouring himself a cup of coffee and taking a sip. "I'm guessing four hours of sleep wasn't adequate."

Rune scrunched his eyebrows as Teagan's head dropped into her hands. "Out all night?"

"Well, let's see," Dad continued, perturbed. "First, your mother is awakened by voices. Naturally, she does what she always does and goes to the rooms of our sons, only to find that Rove is the only one not in his bed or in his room. Second, she wakes me up and I get the wonderful task of coming downstairs and finding your brother, and these two wonderful young ladies, outside in the backyard at three a.m. I figured waking them at seven would play out nicely for what I have planned for them today."

Rove groaned, his spoon dropping into his bowl and milk splashing onto the counter.

"First, you three will clean up the kitchen. Including, mopping the floor." Mom quickly shut off the water pouring into the sink, while a whine escaped Teagan's lips and she promptly slapped a hand over her mouth.

"Second, you will go outside and clean up the wall of the tree house that is spread across the yard, and see if it can be salvaged."

Rove hissed out a breath as Shayne shushed him.

"Third..."

"Come on, Dad," Rove said, exasperated.

"Third," Dad continued as if Rove hadn't said anything. "You and Teagan will compile a list of what we need to fix the wall."

"What's Shayne gonna do?" Rove asked, alarm on his face.

"Since Shayne is the smart one in keeping her comments to herself. She will be released to help the others in searching the books in hopes of finding a way to save Merlin, and your brother, from Kya."

"Oh," Rove answered, handing his dishes to Shayne as she began to stack them.

"That's it?" Dad countered, his coffee cup halfway to his lips. "No back lashed comment or argument?"

"No." Rove stood from his stool taking the dishes from Shayne and carrying them to the sink. He flipped on the water and poured in the soap.

Rune exchanged looks with Roam. This was very unlike their older brother. Even dad and mom exchanged puzzled looks as Rove stuck his hands into the soapy water and began to wash the dishes.

"You three go ahead and get started on the books. It shouldn't take us that long," Rove said, while rinsing off the bowl in his hand and handing it off to Shayne.

"Okay," Rune responded, dragging out the word and standing. He picked up his bowl of cereal and spooned in a mouthful.

"You can finish your breakfast, Rune," Maya said, grabbing her ever-present notebook from off the counter. *"Roam and I can get started."*

He spooned in another bite while filling the bowl with fresh cereal. *"I'm kinda getting used to eating on the run."*

Rune turned, glancing at Mom as he pushed in his stool before heading into the living room. *"I thought you knew these books from cover to cover already, Maya?"* He spooned in another mouthful as he rounded the corner, and saw Riebl bending over their large book.

"Hey!" he yelled, cereal spraying out of his mouth and the bowl spilling as it clattered to the floor. There was no time to even summon an orb. He was flying backwards into the kitchen before he could even think about it, his back slamming into something way too soft to be wood. He rolled to the side and panicked when he saw Maya laying there, blood pooling under her head.

"Maya!" Roam ran towards him while Rove ran past him to the living room. Soapsuds falling to the floor as his flaming ropes appeared, sizzling as the flames hit the water still on his hands. Roam slid to the floor, his hands moving uncertainly as he stared at an unmoving Maya.

"Is she okay?" Rune asked, as Shayne came to kneel beside them, placing a comforting hand on his arm.

"Don't move her!" Dad shouted as he and mom ran toward them, their movements jerking to a sudden halt. Their bodies were frozen in place and Rune knew exactly who was able to do it.

"Kya," he said just seconds before he felt a movement in the air. "Everyone duck!"

A wave of magic swept over his back as Rune's body slumped over Shayne's. He carefully lifted his head to check on everybody else. Rove was in the doorway, slowly inching into the living room. He caught a glimpse of Teagan's sword as it slid around the other side of the doorway and out of sight.

"Go," Shayne said. "Go help Rove and Teagan." She carefully placed a towel around Maya's head, as a scream like no other sounded from the living room.

Rune jumped to his feet, summoning an orb, and turning. Riebl stood, his eyes darting between Kya in an impressive black dress and the doorway where Rune stood. There was no mistaking the redness in the whites of his eyes. Kya was screaming, her hands completely engulfed in purple flames as she held their book. She opened her arms letting their book fall to the carpet as she lifted her eyes and glared in Teagan's direction, just a foot away. With shaking hands, she sneered, touched Riebl with her arm, and they both disappeared.

Rune stood frozen, as everyone else seemed to move at once. He heard the sudden intake of breath, and saw as his parents shook off the residual magic as it dissipated without Kya's presence. Rove ran past him, sweeping his body and dropping down next to where Maya still lay on the floor. Her eyes were still closed, blood soaked into the towel around her head, soaking into her hair. Mom carefully knelt by Maya's head, a first aid kit already conjured into her grasp, while Dad ran to the kitchen and tugged open the drawer where mom kept the kitchen towels. Rune extinguished his orb, running his hand through his hair as he stared at Maya.

"She'll be okay," Teagan assured him, touching his arm briefly before kneeling next to his mom. "I need everyone to back up," she said as she brought her sword forward.

"What are you going to do?" Roam asked, glancing nervously at her sword.

Teagan smiled at Roam. "I want to see if I can heal Maya with my sword like my sword healed me."

"Do you think you can?" Shayne asked, lifting her hands from Maya and sitting back on her heels.

"I don't know, but I think it's worth a try," Teagan responded, looking at Roam.

He nodded, moving back slightly. "Try," he answered his voice catching.

Rune stood, silently praying, as Teagan placed one hand on Maya's head, and lifted her sword with the other. She placed the tip of the sword onto the top of her hand touching Maya. Relief poured through Rune as the sword began to glow. He fell to his knees bending forward, his hands covering his face while tears ran freely down his face.

"Rune?" Dad's voice spoke to him while large hands lifted him to his feet.

"I'm okay," Rune cried as Dad enfolded him and Rune laid his head on his dad's chest. "I'm okay."

"It's not your fault," Dad said, giving him a hug when he cried. "No one thinks that it's your fault."

"I know," Rune answered, unable to stop crying.

Cheering sounded and Rune lifted his head to see Roam take a now awake and fully healed Maya into his arms.

Teagan sat back, smiling. She lifted her sword, said something Rune couldn't understand, and placed the sword to her lips before willing it away.

23

RUNE REACHED DOWN AND PICKED UP SPLINTERED WOOD, TOSSING IT TOWARD the fire pit. Everyone was still inside, awed at how Maya had thought of a spell to place on their book so Kya couldn't take it. It had worked like a charm, except for Kya getting the upper hand and shoving him magically into Maya. Rune knew it wasn't his fault that Maya had gotten hurt. They had both been in the wrong place at the wrong time.

"That new power of yours is going to get annoying if you start disappearing on a regular basis."

Rune chucked another piece of wood towards the pit. "I needed some air," he answered as Roam jumped off the deck and started to help.

"I knew it wasn't your fault," Roam explained as he also threw a piece of wood and missed the pit. "I'm sorry you felt that way."

"I didn't feel that it was my fault, I knew it was Kya's. It doesn't change the fact that it was my body that plowed into Maya's." Rune picked up a bigger piece, chucked it, and it pinged off the pit and flew to thud against the side of the house. "I can't help but think if Teagan's sword hadn't healed Maya we wouldn't be out here cleaning up the yard. And Chuck and Jenna wouldn't be on their way to Ohio."

Rove stepped into the yard, grabbed the slab of wall still intact, and dragged it out of the way. "The way I see it the Magic Council owes us." He reached down and tugged on a broken piece of wood still attached. "I think it's time they helped us take out that psycho freak."

"Magic Council? You think there is one?" Rune asked, jogging over and picking up the pieces that missed the pit. "Just what we need are some white-bearded old codgers staring down at us from up above and analyzing everything we do."

"What makes you think they're up above?" Rove teased, tossing the broken piece to the side.

Roam laughed. "So, replace white-bearded old men to red-bearded old men?"

"Now it just sounds like relatives of Shayne's," Rune joked.

"Oh, well then you would need black, red bearded old men."

Rune looked to the deck, all three girls stood side by side like a united front. "Uh oh," he said chucking the piece still in his hand absently towards the pit. "Am I being ganged up on?"

Maya laughed. "Should've thought of that," she said as she moved to the side of the deck and sat down, letting her legs dangle off the edge and placing her notebook onto her legs.

"Actually, we have something we need to talk to you three about," Teagan mentioned as she and Shayne sat down on either side of Maya, and Rune's brothers came to stand next to him.

"Something that may work in our favor," Shayne added and Rune could swear that Rove stiffened next to him.

"Kya said something to me when Shayne and I were up against her alone," Teagan began, and Rove seemed to relax. "She thinks it's in her favor, but we don't. We think she made a mistake."

"A major mistake," Shayne pointed out her dimples flashing.

"Are we supposed to guess what this mistake is, or are you going to build up for dramatic effect?" Rove questioned, placing a foot on the edge of the deck near Shayne.

Shayne placed her finger on her chin. "Now there's an idea." She laughed when Rove reached down and tickled her thigh. "Okay, okay we'll tell you!"

"Kya referred to the three of us," Teagan said indicating to herself, Maya and Shayne, "As sisters."

"You mean actual sisters?" Roam asked.

Teagan bit her lip. Rune knew it was her way of showing she was nervous. "Yes. She stated that she couldn't believe that we didn't know what was written."

"Wait," Rune held up a hand. "Written where?"

"I don't know. She didn't clarify that."

"How about your book, Maya," Rune asked. "Is there anything in there?"

"Well, there's one reference that I didn't think too much of until now."

"What's the reference, Maya?" Rove asked, crossing his arms across his chest. Rune could swear he saw a flash of purple in his brother's hair. "It's a reference to Mt. Ciadar and its protectors, the Sisters of the Realm."

"That's it?" Rune responded. "That's not much information to go on. What makes you think that it's you three?"

"It's the only thing that would make sense, if Teagan were adopted, that is," Maya answered, swaying her feet.

"What does that have to do with anything?" Roam questioned.

"Maya and Shayne were both adopted. If I was too, then it would make sense that we were all the daughters of the Sorceress of the Sun."

"So, you're thinking that the daughters of the Sorceress of the Sun would be these Sisters of the Realm," Rune clarified. "Are you sure you're not adopted, Teagan?"

"Absolutely," Teagan answered reaching into her back pocket and pulling out a small wallet. She opened it and extracted a picture handing it off to Rune.

"That's a picture of my dad and me," Teagan explained as the brothers took a look.

"He's definitely your dad," Rune stated, handing the picture back.

"What about your mom?" Roam asked.

"Her picture is back at Vlad's castle," she explained. "I'm not very proud to show off the parent who abandoned me."

"So, if you don't think you are actual sisters, then how can this information be in our favor?" Rune questioned.

"Because," Maya began looking toward the other two girls. "We think she may have gotten the reference wrong."

"You're doing it again," Rove said, agitated. "Spit it out already."

Maya laughed. "We think the reference was to the actual sisters."

Rove rolled his eyes and began picking up the last of the wood pieces still in the yard. "So, she got her reference wrong. How is that supposed to be in our favor?" He stood long enough to make air quotations over the last two words.

"That's where you three come in," Shayne replied, smiling sweetly.

"Huh?" Rove responded mid-swing. "What does *that* mean?"

Maya looked to Roam. "We need the three of you to connect like you did to find me in the cave."

Rune's eyes lifted in surprise. "Because?"

"Because you're going to contact Merlin."

"Hurry up!"

Riebl leafed slowly through the book of black magic. How was he supposed to find what she wanted in here when he couldn't even read what it said?

"What are you, illiterate?" she panted, with her hands extended straight off her lap as she sat in one of the chairs brought down from the kitchen.

Riebl stopped, leaning against the table and cocking his head toward her. "Illiterate isn't a factor when something is written in another language!" he responded, his voice rising. "If you keep throwing insults out at me, I'm not going to help you and your hands can stay a charred mess."

A growl escaped her lips. "I'm sorry," she spat. "This is extremely painful and I would like to fix it. Please hurry up and find the spell."

"What's in it for me if I do as you ask?"

Kya's eyes, filled with pain and anger, lifted. "If you help me," she responded through gritted teeth. "I won't kill you."

Riebl's eyebrows lifted in shock. "Not now, not ever?"

Kya's eyes took on a look of total hatred as a snarl appeared at the corner of her mouth. "Yes. I will not kill you now, or ever. Happy now?" She looked at him with an insincere smile. "Find the spell before I change my mind."

Riebl quickly turned back to the book. He turned pages, always mindful of the three candles burning which allowed him access to these dark pages. He scanned page after page looking for the specific look Kya told him to watch for. He turned another page and there it was. His hands shook as he contemplated not telling her, but his want to stay alive and get away from this book was stronger. "I found it," he said, carefully stepping away from the book so she could stand in his place.

He moved back into the dark recess of the room, watching as she chanted in a long forgotten language. Blackness seeped out of the book to twirl first over the open pages of the book, and then reached out to her to surround her as she continued to chant. Wind slapped at him pushing him back against the wall. Blackness traveled to the ceiling reminding him of a tornado as it spun with Kya in its center, picking up speed. His eyes widened when he saw Kya shrouded in the deepest blackness he had ever seen. Her hair slapped and twisted, spiraling in the air the blackness created. She raised her arms, the blackness completely covering where her hands should have been, her chanting growing louder until his eardrums felt as if they would pop. Riebl shielded his eyes as black lightning flashed once, shadows filling the room making him shudder as he got a firsthand look at the evil living within the pages of this book. Eyes surrounded with an empty abyss stared directly at him, an evil smile appearing, which he was certain was meant for only him.

Riebl shook as the blackness dissipated, seeping back into the pages of the book. He suddenly knew this book was meant as a tomb for this darkness, and Kya was allowing it freedom each time she used it. He shuddered as Kya turned her cured hands in the air.

"So much better," she said as she carefully closed the book and blew out the candles. "Thank you, Riebl."

He stood pressed against the wall, fear overtaking his body.

"Is that anyway to respond when someone thanks you?" Kya asked as she turned toward him and blackness flashed in eyes that were once green.

"You're...you're welcome, Kya," he answered inching away from the wall to move towards the door.

She began to pace, blocking his path making him stop. She laughed, the sound almost foreign, as she flattened her hand and a long bladed knife appeared. "They think they have won," she said as she ran her fingers down the blade. "They think they have taken me out of commission for a time." She turned to face him, her face looking more hideous than before with black lines filling creases. "Won't they be surprised then when my completed army takes them down!" She threw back her head and laughed as Riebl covered his already damaged ears.

Her laughter stopped suddenly and she spun towards him, flashes of black appearing in her eyes, her excitement growing. "Go to the kitchen and grab the glass measuring cup from the cupboard. Then meet me at Merlin's cell."

"What is the measuring cup for?" Riebl asked, his heart beating a staccato in his chest, threatening to break free.

"I need the wizard's blood to expand my army. Go! Now!"

Riebl skirted the wall to the doorway and shot out into the hall. He never looked back as he ran hearing Kya's last words.

"This is going to be so much fun!"

24

HE HAD EXPECTED TO SEE AN OLD DERELICT BARN, READY TO FALL IN ON ITSELF if the wind blew in just the right direction. But the barn roof he landed on was solid and strong. Rune placed his hands on his hips and looked over at overgrown fields.

"Not what you were expecting?"

He looked at Teagan and smiled. "No, this suits you. It's the sturdy barn I wasn't expecting." He glanced over the side, then back at Teagan and winked. "How's the hayloft?"

Teagan raised an eyebrow. "The hayloft?"

He drew her into his arms. "Anyone ever show you the many uses of a hayloft?"

"Ewwww!" Shayne exclaimed, jumping from foot to foot, as she put on her flip-flops. "TMI, Rune. TMI!"

"Like Rove wasn't thinking the same thing." He ducked, laughing, and somehow avoided Rove cuffing him on the back of his head.

"I can see why you come here," Maya said as she turned looking around. "It's beautiful here, and private. I'm sorry we've invaded your secret haven."

"It's okay," Teagan answered. "You're not invading anything. I'm happy to share with friends."

Roam walked to the peak of the roof and sat down. "If we're gonna do this thing, let's do it before I change my mind."

"Why would you change your mind?" Rove asked joining Roam. "You've done this before."

Roam scratched his head. "Yeah, but we don't know if Pappy is on this plane or a mythical one."

"You think there's a difference?" Rune asked, sitting across from his brothers.

"Don't you?" Roam countered, repositioning himself.

"No," Rune answered placing his hands palm up on his knees. "We're magical beings. We should be able to go anywhere we want to."

"I hope you're right," Roam said, placing his hand into Rune's.

"If you're having doubts, this may not work." Rove looked uncomfortably at his brother.

"It's not really doubt. What if I can't find him?"

"That's doubt," Rove answered. "You've done this before, Roam. You can do this."

"How exactly does this work?" Teagan asked sitting down next to Rune.

"The prophecy stated that I could hear all and not be heard. When Maya went missing, I tested the prophecy by concentrating on just her. I was able to hear her and her surroundings."

"When we were running out of time, we all linked and Roam was able to see Maya in the cave," Rove added.

"You're stronger together. We've all witnessed that," Shayne said as she sat next to Rove.

Maya knelt next to Roam and placed her hands on each side of his face. "You can do this. I have complete faith in you."

Roam nodded. "Let's do this."

"Oh, and ladies?" Rove moved to sit closer to Rune. "Just so you know, this will take a while, and Roam will be able to hear everything you say."

"And if you talk too much or too loud he might yell at you in your mind. And believe me, it hurts worse than when he gives a mind zap." Rune added.

"Good to know," Teagan responded, planting a kiss on Rune's lips and scooting back.

Rune turned his head and smiled at her. "When we're done here, you and I will go check out that hayloft."

"Get your mind out of the gutter and concentrate," Rove ordered squeezing his hand.

"All right, all right!" Rune yanked his hand away and rubbed his head. "I'll concentrate! Stop it, Roam!"

Roam laughed, reaching out and retaking Rune's hand in his.

Rune closed his eyes and shook his head to relieve the last of the mind zap pain from his head. Last time, Maya's life was on the line and it was easier for him to concentrate. This time, he knew that Teagan was just an arm's length away and she was probably looking right at him. He peeked through one eye and instead of seeing his girlfriend, he saw Rove glaring at him. Chuckling to himself, he closed his eyes again and this time concentrated until he began to scream.

TEAGAN RAN her hands up and down her arms, keeping her footsteps light as she moved closer to Maya. "I know they said it would take a while," she whispered. "But this is taking longer than I expected."

Maya looked at her watch. "It's only been fifteen minutes. Let's not get nervous until it reaches thirty minutes."

"Too late," Shayne whispered back, starting to rock. "I'm way past nervous and heading towards neurotic." She was sitting on the roof with her knees pulled tight to her body.

"Something's happening," Teagan said, as she darted a look between Shayne and Roam. They were the only two who seemed affected by whatever was happening. No movement came from Rove or Rune. Maya touched her arm with a hand just as Rune and Rove's screams shattered the silence. Teagan and Maya both jumped and Shayne's hands shot to her own ears, a scream shrieking out as she rocked her body faster. Teagan dropped down next to her friend as Maya ran to kneel between Rune and Rove, placing a hand on each of their shoulders.

"What's happening?" Teagan demanded, removing Shayne's hands from her ears and trying to keep her voice calm.

"A barrier! Kya has a barrier!" Shayne gasped out, her hands locked in Teagan's. Her eyes opened holding pain and fear as she looked back at her friend, her breathing quickening and her body shaking. "It has a hold of Rune and Rove's mind. It hurts, Teagan."

"How do you know?" Maya questioned.

"Remember, Shayne can't close the door to telepathy. She can hear everything and apparently she can feel it too!" Teagan reminded. She hugged Shayne close to her feeling her friend's body quivering. "Breathe through it, Shay. Can you see or hear anything?"

"I can hear Roam," she remarked, her voice an octave higher. "Roam's trying to help them. He's saying something about a web-like barrier and this one Rove can't get out of."

"You have to try and see, Shay. There has to be something you can do to help them."

Maya's eyes shot to Teagan's. "Are you crazy? It could trap Shayne too and we won't be able to get any of them out!"

"And if Shayne doesn't try, we could lose all of them forever."

Teagan turned, the space on the roof diminishing as the boys' family, and Diego, landed one by one. Maya moved closer to Roam as the rest dispersed themselves around all of them. Adrianna coming to Shayne, kneeling down next to her and taking her face in her hands.

"I see you took matters into your own hands again," Dimitri said, kneeling next to Maya and Roam.

"Not now, Dimitri," Adrianna ordered. "Shayne, honey, can you help Roam?"

"I think so," Shayne replied, her body shaking more than before. "I need to be closer to him."

Shayne's hand shook when she lifted it to touch Roam on the side of his head, once he was within reach. As soon as Shayne touched him, her back arched and a scream tore from her lips. As tears streamed down her face, she took in a deep breath and her body shuddered.

"I don't like this," Teagan said loudly, peering over her friend to look into Adrianna's eyes. "She's never done anything like this before. We need to get her out."

"No!" Shayne shouted, making Teagan's eyes go wide in shock. "I think I know what to do."

"You think?" Maya questioned, fear in her eyes.

Shayne's teeth clenched and sweat poured down her face to mix with her tears. "Don't let them let go. I need them to stay connected until I'm sure."

Dimitri clamped a hand over one of Roam's hands as Maya did the same with the other. Vlad and Aradney secured Rove's, as Radek and Francesca followed suit with Rune. They all looked to one another with questioning looks as either Rune or Rove let out yells of pain. Teagan looked up as Diego came to sit next to her, placing an arm around her. She rested her head on his shoulder as she watched her dearest friend fight to keep her composure.

"Shayne has the power of premonition. That's power of the mind," Diego said. "If anyone can do this, it's Shayne. Doubting her isn't going to help anyone."

"But Teagan said so herself, she's never done this before," Maya responded with panic in her voice.

"Just as all of you have never dealt with what you have been handed," Adrianna reminded. "We have to let Shayne try, just as we have had to let you try."

Maya nodded, wiping away tears as they fell on their own accord, looking to Roam.

"I've almost got it," Shayne said, more relaxed, a small smile creeping across her lips.

"Just for the record, this wasn't my idea."

Teagan's head spun. Rune's eyes were opened, but heavily lidded, he looked at her and gave her a weak smile. He leaned into Radek, his arms going limp.

"Don't let him break the connection!" Adrianna reminded. "Not until we get them all out safely!"

"I guess that would be me too," Rove said, his voice weak. He slowly turned his head until his eyes settled on Shayne.

"No, you don't!" Vlad exclaimed, holding Rove down. "Not yet. Your mom is watching over Shayne while she helps get you all out. Stay put."

Teagan felt completely helpless. Never before had she seen her friend do what she was doing now. Teagan wished there was something she could do to help get her and Roam out from wherever they were. Shayne's body began to sag and Teagan quickly placed a hand behind her back. She quickly glanced to Roam; his eyes were struggling to open, his body beginning to loosen. With a loud sigh, Shayne's hand dropped and Diego caught her as she fell backward. Roam's body fell forward, the connection breaking between the three brothers as hands reached out to grab him.

"Roam? Roam? You okay?" Dimitri called concerned.

"Shayne," Roam responded.

"We got her," Dimitri answered, his voice hitching.

Roam shook his head. "She's still in," he said weakly.

Rove moved unsteadily, batting away Vlad's hand as he crawled to where Shayne lay motionless in Diego's lap. He shook his head when Diego began to lift her.

"It's okay," he said, his voice sounding weak. He took Shayne's hand in his and gently turned her head to face his while he leaned heavily against his mom. "C'mon baby. You gotta come back now."

Shayne stirred. Her eyes flying open. The gray in her eyes moving like storm clouds, becoming more intense while her pupils dilated.

"What's happening?" Rove asked, alarmed.

Teagan got on her knees, grabbing Shayne's other hand. "She's having a vision."

"How long do they last?" Rove questioned.

"It depends," Teagan answered, running her fingers down the side of Shayne's cheek.

"Depends on what?" Rune asked, sitting down heavily next to Teagan.

"On the vision and what she's meant to see."

"And then we get her back?" Rove asked, sounding more panicked than before.

Teagan looked at him. "Hopefully."

Teagan tried to remain calm. She could hear Maya's watch ticking out the minutes as she stared at Shayne silently wishing for her friend to come back. For what seemed like forever, Shayne's eyes finally flicked their usual gray color. Her pupils began to retract and her eyelids finally fluttered until she took in a struggling breath and stared up at Rove.

"There's so many!" Shayne cried, her eyes tearing up. "We can't possibly fight them all, Rove!"

"It's okay, Shayne." He gently wiped away her tears. "We'll figure it out."

"You don't understand!" Shayne sat up in Diego's lap grabbing onto the front of Rove's shirt with both hands. "Kya's gonna make more of those beings!"

"Calm down, okay?" Rove placed his hands on Shayne's. "We'll figure out what we need to do."

"No!" Shayne tore her hands away and stood. "Listen to me!" she begged, emphasizing with her hands. "Kya has a book. An old black book. She lights candles before she opens it. Two black and one white. She takes Merlin's blood and uses the book to make more of those black beings!" Her eyes sought out Teagan as she wheezed in a breath. "She will know that Rune is the key, not just the one with the key, but the key itself. Rune *is* the *key!*"

Shayne lost her composure then, grabbing onto Teagan, her eyes wild and her voice hysterical. "Kya's going to come here and while we fight the black beings she's going to take Rune, Teagan!"

Teagan turned her head as she tried to console her friend, seeking out the only one who could help Shayne now. Vlad caught her eye and nodded once. He waved a hand in Shayne's direction, Rove helping to catch her as she fell.

"Let's go back to the house," Adrianna suggested, her voice subdued. "We'll let Shayne and the boys rest. Then we'll figure out what we need to do."

Vlad scooped Shayne up into his arms, looking to Teagan before taking to the sky. If Shayne meant the battle was going to happen at the barn, Teagan swore none of them would ever return.

25

BACK AND FORTH, MERLIN PACED, TOYING WITH THE BANDS BOUND AROUND his wrists. He no longer knew what the date was, or whether it was day or night. His heart felt as if it were breaking as he thought of his family and whether or not they were in peril. He yanked on each of his bands, knowing fully they would never break under his fingers, but his want to be free was so strong he tried anyway. He closed his eyes as grief and blame filled his mind, letting his head fall back and opening his eyes to see the dingy ceiling and a shadow creep across its space. His eyes widened just before he slowly brought them down to see Riebl standing beside his cage, a finger to his lips.

He stared at the nightwalker, not knowing what to do, as Riebl brought his other hand around and dangled a paper from his fingertips just inside the bars. When Merlin didn't move, Riebl shook the paper and motioned for him to take it. Slowly, Merlin walked to the bars and took the offered paper from the nightwalker's grasp, bringing it to his eyes so he could read the written message it contained.

Don't talk she's listening. How do I destroy the book?

Merlin lifted his eyes, mimicking writing and waited for the nightwalker to produce a pencil. He brought the pencil to the paper and jumped back when the paper alighted with fire and he dropped it onto the floor of his cell. He snapped his head up in Riebl's direction in time to see the nightwalker fly into the vacant cell across from his and slam into the wall. As Riebl crumpled to the floor, the cell door slammed shut and Kya appeared.

"Idiot," she said as she spit in Riebl's direction. "I should've put you in there long ago." She glanced to Merlin, a smile playing across her black painted lips.

"Handy little spell, wouldn't you say?" she asked, her hips sashaying in her snuggly fit dress. "Too bad I won't need it any longer." Kya waved a hand absently towards Riebl. He cried out as blackness floated from him to dissolve in the air above his head.

Merlin stood in the center of his cell, his arms dangling at his sides. He followed Kya with his eyes to keep her within his sight. He lifted his head and squared his shoulders, only taking a step back when blackness swirled around her eyes, which used to be green. Her hair was almost entirely black, with only streaks of red remaining, the ends moving as if Medusa had borrowed out her hair of snakes. If he was going to die, he was going to go down with every ounce of strength he had left.

Kya stopped a foot from his cell and scrunched her nose at him. "You smell, old man. Even the rats would stay away from you with that hideous stench." She lifted her hand and snapped her fingers.

A wave of magic traveled across Merlin's skin. He had no choice but to tear his eyes away from the sorceress to look upon his own tattered robe. He lifted his arms and stared as his robe repaired itself, the stitches becoming whole. His mangled beard untangled itself and turned white once again, while his skin tingled and filth disappeared. The magic left him to travel across the cell, grime and dirt leaving as if someone was scrubbing it away. Very slowly, he turned to look into Kya's black, coated eyes. He stilled his body from retracting as this mistress of black magic brought her hands up and grasped onto the bars.

"It is always necessary to say thank you when someone does something nice for another."

Merlin wet his lips before responding. "Thank you, Kya. I appreciate being clean again."

She tilted her head and snickered. "If only I had done it for you." One finger lifted and wagged at him. Merlin didn't even try fighting, knowing it wouldn't do him any good. He only braced himself for the impact, which would follow, but was surprised when he only bumped into the bars and a tsk left Kya's lips.

"Stupid nightwalker forgot to bring me my measuring cup," she said, snapping her fingers. A measuring cup appeared to float beside her while she grabbed onto his arm and pulled it through the bars. "I would say this will only hurt a little, but I would be lying." With a sneer across her lips, Kya took her nail and cut the length of his forearm.

Merlin cried out. The pain was worse than he could even imagine. The measuring cup floated under his arm, just as the vial had done the last time Kya had taken his blood. He tried not to panic when his blood filled to the two cup mark, then vanished. Kya took her thumb, pressing down on his open wound. Merlin's knees buckled, pain tearing into his entire body and bringing him to his knees. With cackling laughter, Kya freed him from his torture. Merlin lifted his head and with tear filled eyes stared at the Mistress of Darkness.

"I am now your superior," she said as blackness swirled around her. "Once my army destroys all who stand against me and I gain the book and key, I will return for you to take me to the Enchanted Realm where I will reign and have dominion over all." With a flash of blackness, Kya disappeared, leaving behind Riebl who still lay lifeless in his cell.

Merlin let his head drop to the floor of his cell. Gut wrenching sobs left him as he cried for the ones who would suffer next.

"TELL us about the book you saw," Mom said as she sat on the coffee table and placed a hand on one of Shayne's thighs.

Rune took the spot next to Teagan leaning forward and placing his arms on his thighs. Everyone was here, either sitting or standing as his mom quietly encouraged Shayne to speak of the vision she saw on the roof of the barn over two hours ago. Rune's gaze stopped when he reached Rove,

153

sitting next to Shayne. There was no mistaking the anger and concern displayed on his oldest brother's face.

Shayne tucked a stray hair behind her ear with shaking fingers. "It's large," she began, her voice soft as she wrung her hands in her lap until Rove stilled them with one of his own. She turned one hand upward and clasped onto his as she continued to stare at the carpet.

"It's a charred black with an inverted silver star on the cover. Kya lights three candles, one white and two black. She says something I don't quite hear as she lights them all at once with only the wave of her fingers, then opens the book. The pages are slightly black around the edges when she first opens it, and then the blackness spreads across the pages turning them completely black. Words in Old Latin begin to glow off the pages. Kya then grabs a smaller book and opens it. It looks like a personal journal at first because it is hand written, but when I looked closer it had words written in Old Latin with a translation in English."

"Obviously, Kya can't read Latin," Roam declared, flicking blue streaked hair out of his eyes.

"What does the page say that she is deciphering?" Maya asked.

"The page reads, 'How to Make an Army.'"

"I think we have already been introduced to her supposed army and Teagan was able to demolish them," Rune said proudly.

"That doesn't mean she can't build it stronger," Shayne replied. "The book she is using has to be black magic, since no good magic would look like this."

"You said something about Merlin and Kya taking his blood," Roam reminded her. "Where does that fall into this?"

Shayne wet her lips and cleared her throat. "Everything I see is jumbled. You can't rely on what I see as to how it happens and it isn't complete."

"We aren't going to blame you of how it falls into place," Teagan answered. "We just need details on how to hopefully stop Kya."

"You can't stop her," Shayne pleaded, finally looking up with tears welling in her eyes. "Merlin is in a cell, in what looks like a dungeon. Kya takes her nail and cuts open Merlin's skin. His blood flows into a large measuring cup and doesn't stop until it's full. When Kya's at the book, the beings begin to appear all around her."

Rove takes both of Shayne's hands in his and smiles when she looks at him. "Try and picture Kya at the book. Is the cup of blood there?"

Shayne closed her eyes and nodded before opening them again. "Yes, it's there on the other side of the book."

"Okay, the book is there and the blood. When does Kya realize that Rune is the key?"

Rune held his breath as Shayne closed her eyes again. He wanted to tell Rove he was doing great, but remembered in time that Shayne would hear him telepathically.

Shayne's eyes snap back open. "When Kya touches the blood, that's when she knows."

"Like a vision?" Vlad asks.

Shayne's head nods frantically. "Yes, that's it. Like a vision. Kya has a vision!"

"Okay," Rove says, softening his voice. "You said there's a battle. Where are we then?"

Shayne's lower lip trembled. "She takes Rune."

"I know," Rove says, he grabs her face in-between his hands and wipes away tears with his thumbs. "You have to see past that. Where are we when the next battle begins?"

Tears streamed down Shayne's face, her body shaking. "I don't know. There are so many black beings I can't tell where we are."

Disappointment showed on Rove's face as he pulled Shayne in to rest her head on his shoulder. He looked directly at Rune. "It's okay. We won't worry about it. We'll have to make sure we are with Rune at all times."

"But we are," Shayne says as Rove shushes her. "We can't stop her, Rove! It's not going to matter if we know where it happens and change the location. She's still going to come and she's still going to get Rune!"

Rove looked up until his eyes rested on Vlad. His grandfather moved forward and Shayne's head snapped up.

"Don't you dare!" Shayne warned, pointing a finger at him. "And don't even think of doing it with your mind either. Whatever I saw is going to happen soon, I can feel it. I need to be able to help and I can't do that if you keep knocking me out and making my head feel fuzzy."

Vlad runs a hand down his face and nods. "Okay, I won't for now. In the meantime, we need to get a plan together. We may not be ahead of Kya, but because of Shayne we know what she's going to do. We need to figure out how to keep Rune from her evil clutches and get Merlin back."

"Shayne's right," Mom adds and waits as all heads turn towards her. "It isn't going to matter where the location is when she takes Rune, we need to be ready."

"I need some air." Rune stands from the couch only to be stopped by Teagan.

"Not alone," she says. "We're all going with you."

"I'll get a barrier in place," Maya added. "At least we know Kya can't break through it, or at least she hasn't been able to so far."

Rove grabs a hold of Rune's arm. "Get used to us being around. You don't go anywhere without at least two of us. Got it?"

"Yeah, I got it." Rune placed his hand in Teagan's and began walking towards the back door. His brothers and Maya right behind him.

2 6

Darkness surrounded her, swirling and grasping onto her clothing, her hair and limbs. It whispered past her ear, giving comfort as it snuggled against her body like a companion. Kya welcomed it into her mind, body and soul as she stood before the book of ultimate darkness. She smiled, running her hands down the cover of the book. Such power this book contained, such promise! She would soon have everything she deserved and more.

She reached out with the pointer finger of her right hand, her razor sharp black nail extending much farther than her finger. With only a thought, flame flew from her nail, lighting the white candle in the center, then the two black simultaneously. She watched as the flames shot towards the ceiling before settling. Only then did she grasp the cover of the book and carefully open it.

She loved to watch the pages turn from an old, faded black to a deep charcoal. Her smile widening as the words began to glow in Old Latin. Carefully, always mindful of the flickering flames, she turned the pages until she reached the one she recognized and trailed her nail down the page. Slowly, she brought down the accompanying book and checked the translation before allowing excitement to course through her veins. This was it. This was how the fight will turn in her favor.

Kya grabbed the measuring cup filled with her most precious ingredient. With one pinkie, she swirled the red liquid, running her finger on the side of the cup as her mind began to cloud, and her eyes became unfocused. Light took the place of darkness while images invaded her space and a vision began.

At first, it was like an old silent movie showing glimpses of the Gustavos and their entourage. The vision flicked between the brothers with faces exactly like the other, before settling on only one with white streaks in his raven hair. She watched as the vision showed him picking up what appeared to be a necklace on the floor of the cave she had once stayed in. The same necklace falling to the ground out of the pocket of the same brother, only to be picked up by another with blue streaks. The same boy with white streaked hair standing next to the others as a Latin word is burned in a piece of wood, and the necklace reappearing from under the shirt of this same brother, dangling next to the Gustavo crest. The vision changed suddenly, showing a passageway she didn't recognize. She watched as she took the necklace from the boy, and placed its pendant onto a pedestal with some kind of design carved into its center, but nothing happened. She made the boy do it and a gate appeared.

Kya blinked as the vision faded and returned her to the present. She quickly flipped through her book with Latin words translated into English. A smile crept across her face as she read the meaning of the word burned into the wood. The brother with the white streaks in his raven hair had the key, and he was the only one who could turn it. Her smile widened more when she realized this boy wasn't just the holder of the key, he *was* the key.

THE DAY WAS BEGINNING to fade as Rune looked off into the tree line. It ticked him off that he was scanning, looking for any signs that Kya was near, but no inky blackness was creeping across the ground, or hanging out above the trees. All he saw was the outline of Maya's translucent purple barrier enveloping part of the forest and his home. He wasn't sure if he was relieved or not, and didn't have time to dwell on it when something grabbed his leg and held fast. Rune then turned and glared at his oldest brother.

"Really, Rove?"

"Hey, it looked like you were checking for an escape route. I had to make sure you stayed put."

"That's a good idea," Rune responded, smirking, and disappeared, only to feel a tug on his leg and he reappeared landing hard on his side on the deck.

"That didn't work," Rove commented, reaching down a hand to pull Rune to his feet. "I told you, you're not going anywhere without any of us."

"That's not what I was doing," Rune answered, exasperated. "I wanted to see if I could transport out of your grasp."

"Why?" Rove questioned.

"So when Kya grabs me I can get away."

Rove ran a hand through his hair making red streaks stand on end. "I knew what you were going to do, but Kya wouldn't. That's a pretty good idea. It might work."

"Wouldn't hurt to do some trial runs," Roam suggested.

"You willing to get a little bruised up?" Teagan asked, a corner of her mouth tilting upward.

"Is that a promise?" Rune joked, just before Shayne gasped. One minute, Rune was standing on the deck, the next he was flying off it in the grasp of his oldest brother. They both landed on the ground with a grunt.

"You're making this way too easy, Rune," Rove grunted, putting Rune in a headlock. "You can try any..."

There was a slight snap to the air and Rune awkwardly rematerialized on the deck. He nodded his head, brushing dirt off his clothes. "Okay, it worked. Not exactly the way I had planned, but it worked."

"You're going to need to get better," Roam said just before blue lightning shot out of his fingertips hitting the deck at Rune's feet.

Rune yelped, jumping back only to be stopped by a purple barrier.

"What is this? You're all going to gang up on me?"

Roam lowered his hands and Maya retracted her barrier. "You can't know when it's going to happen. Otherwise, you won't transport out on a whim."

"And you already failed," Maya countered. "You have to be able to act quickly if you want this to work."

"Alright, I get it," Rune answered running a hand through his hair. "Let's try this..."

A red-scaled rope wrapped around his leg and pulled him off the deck. Rune slapped a hand down on the ground in frustration. He had to work harder. He concentrated, willing his body to transport and landed softly on the ground just in front of the tree house. This time he used his sensing power as feelers to the next attack, and, to his surprise, Rune felt a pulse to his right where Roam was. He transported just seconds before lightning hit the ground at his feet. He landed softly again, this time on the deck and felt a pulse. Teagan stepped in front of him, a sword in each hand.

"Whoa, you hold on," Rune exclaimed, bringing his hands up palms out. "I'm not going to fight with you and your sword. No matter how many you hold."

Teagan smiled, twirling one sword as she planted her feet apart. "I'm not going to hurt you. It's just for effect. They know you're not a threat, but I wouldn't recommend you use your power though, just in case."

Rune gulped. "What effect are we going for here? See if you can get me to scream like a girl?"

"Works for me."

Rune turned just in time to have a bat fly in his face. His first response was to swat at it, but instead he ignored it and transported to land just inside the tree house. A barrier shot out behind him, smacking him in the back, and knocking him out the gaping hole where the wall used to be. Instead of landing on the ground, Rune transported to the sky where he hovered until fire wrapped around him and pulled him to the ground.

"Rune!"

Feet thundered as he tried to catch his breath, while hands flipped him onto his side.

"Did I burn you, Rune? Rune, you okay?"

"I'm fine. Stop pawing me!" Rune swatted away hands and sat up. "Seriously, I'm fine!"

"I didn't mean to grab you. I only put it to flame to scare you." Rove grabbed his shirt and yanked it up.

"Rove, stop! I'm fine. No burns. Look! My clothes aren't even burned!"

Rove plopped down on the ground, scrubbing his hands down his face. "I think you might want to try that again."

Rune turned his head and glared at his centuries old grandfather. "Say again?"

Vlad smirked, going down on his haunches next to him. "Rove thought he burned Shayne, remember? She was fine then too. Maybe there is a safety mechanism between all of you. Maybe you can use your powers on each other. Maybe you can use your powers when one is in trouble."

Rune rolled, jumping to his feet. He transported to the sky and hovered, just like before. "Roam, hit me!" he shouted down.

Roam stared back at him, shaking his head. "I don't know about this."

"If I'm wrong, Teagan can heal him," Vlad said, smacking Roam on the shoulder. "It's the only way we are going to know. Hit him with your best shot."

"Really, a Pat Benetar reference?" Rove asked, coming to stand beside them.

"Don't knock a good song," Vlad answered, beginning to hum.

Roam looked up and Rune shrugged. He wasn't really sure how he felt about getting hit with lightning, but they did have a healer. Somehow, that didn't make his nerves ease any. Rune watched as Roam lifted his hands up. He clamped his teeth together and braced himself for the hit as blue lightning shot out of his brother's fingertips. Lightning danced across his skin and clothes, but no pain what-so-ever.

"I think Vlad might be right," Rune called down. "I can feel it and see it, but it doesn't hurt!"

"Brace yourself, Rune," Roam called back.

Before Rune could answer, full power lightning hit him. He felt pressure hit his body, veering him off course, but not knocking him out of the sky. He looked down his body covered in a haze of blue and laughed.

"Maybe you're frying him to a pulp, Roam," Rove said. "Teagan might not be able to heal pulp."

"I'm fine," Rune said. He transported to the ground, grabbing Rove excitedly by the arm. "Your turn, fire me up!"

"Are you crazy?"

"You're right, we already covered that." Rune turned to Teagan, splaying his arms wide. "Stab me."

"No way," Teagan answered, her swords disappearing from her hands.

"You've lost your mind," Rove said, swinging Rune back around. "Roam's power must have fried your brain cells! Teagan's swords may be magical, but they're real. If she stabs you, you'll have a real stab wound."

"Maya didn't hurt me. Roam didn't and neither did you and all our powers are real," Rune said, pointing to each of them. "Why would her swords be any different? Just as you said, they're magical."

"Like Rove said, the swords are real," Mom said as she brought Excalibur into her grasp. She faced Dad and nodded. Dad ran his hand down the blade of Excalibur, wincing, as blood poured where the sword cut him. "Excalibur won't cut me because I am its protector. But it will hurt others, magical or not. It's real."

"But you didn't cut one of us," Rune argued. "We're the magical beings we have to test this against, not Dad."

"Why do we have to test if a sword cuts you or not?" Rove argued back. "It's not like Kya is going to grab Excalibur or the Great Smith's sword. She can't."

Rune dragged a hand through his hair. "Alright, I got a little carried away. You're right. It's not like Teagan is going to stab any of us during a fight. If Kya or Riebl use a sword, it's going to cut and it's going to hurt."

"While we are on the subject of Kya and Riebl," Dad said, as Teagan healed his hand. "Mom and I have been talking inside while you've all been abusing Rune. We think we should somehow call Kya out and lead her toward the barn. It's away from the house and the general population. We could end this there once and for all."

"Kya will take Rune," Shayne responded running her hands up and down her arms. "I've seen it."

"That doesn't mean it's going to happen, or that we can't prevent it from happening," Rove answered going to her. "You were given that vision for a reason, so that we can stop Kya and keep Rune safe."

"But what if..."

Rune went to her, taking Shayne by the hands. "I know what you saw, and I appreciate how worried you are about me. But I think Rove is right.

You were given that vision for a reason so we can change the outcome. We have to try."

Shayne looked to each of them and then squeezed Rune's hands. "Okay, let's do this your way. But please, let's make sure we have a plan before bringing Kya to the barn."

"Absolutely," Vlad said, taking to the sky. "I'll get the others."

27

Whatever he was leaning against was hard and cold as Riebl slowly opened his eyes to be greeted by the bars of his cell. Panic overtook him, making him scurry to his feet and grab onto the cold steel bars. He attempted to shake them while staring across at the wizard sitting silent and still. "What am I doing in here?"

Merlin's head lifted from where he sat on his cement bed. "Kya put you there. She knew what you were trying to do and imprisoned you."

"Get me out of here!" Riebl yelled, pulling on the door of his cell. "I don't belong here. Get me out!"

"And how do you presume I do that?" Merlin asked angrily, getting off his bed and coming to stand in front of the bars. "Should I magically make these go away?" He thrust his hands through the bars turning his wrists to show his black bands.

Riebl raked his fingers through his long hair, his eyes darting nervously around the silent dungeon. "She promised she wouldn't kill me."

"Oh, I've kept my promise. You're not dead yet."

A swirl of black appeared between the cells, twisting ever so slightly before Kya came into view. She was still wearing her newly conjured black dress, her feet were still bare. When she turned to gaze in his direction, Riebl stepped back. More black lines filled creases of her face, while blackness had overtaken her red hair. Blackness clung to her as if it were a part of her, reaching out in different directions, as if tasting the air for something it wanted. Riebl shook, hoping it wouldn't be him, stepping back away from his barred door.

"I need a warrior," she said as the door of his cell swung open.

Riebl kept his distance from the opening. There was no way he was going out there. "I'm no warrior," he said, shaking his head and backing up until he was stopped by the cold cement wall. "Get one of the Gustavos to do your bidding."

"All in due time," Kya answered. She lifted her hand and before Riebl knew what was happening, he was floating out the cell doors toward her.

"No!" Riebl yelled, grabbing onto the bars only to have them ripped from his clutches. "No, Kya. You promised!"

"Oh, come now," Kya jeered. He stopped inches from her to be placed on the grey cement floor. She ran her fingers down his cheek. "As I said, I need a warrior and you'll have to do."

His cell door banged shut, and Riebl nearly fainted. Nothing good could come of this, nothing. Kya snapped her fingers and a dagger coated in blackness appeared in front of him. He stared. It was magnificent, with its blade curving like a snake and floating just above his right hand as if to taunt him.

"Take it," she said. "You know you want to."

He did want to. He shook his head trying to keep reason but his judgment was cloudy.

"Take it, either way you will have to fight."

Riebl looked away from the dagger to watch Kya take three steps backwards and lean back against the stone wall of the dungeon. "Fight? Fight what?"

She smiled, her eyes glittering with excitement, as she lifted both hands and twisted them in the air. Darkness left her to float across the ceiling like fog on a dark and deserted road. It began to thicken, taking on consistency, only to begin to drip from the ceiling and slither down the walls.

Riebl backed up, the dagger following his movement, as drop after drop landed at his feet and began to take on form. His eyes grew wide as black beings began to grow from the cement floor and taking steps toward him.

He looked to where their faces should be and shuddered at their empty abyss of creepy blackness. Riebl looked to the dagger, then to the beings multiplying in numbers. She had given him no choice. Riebl reached a hand out and grasped the hilt of the dagger. It was light and awkward, nothing like the one the girl had taken from him. Just the thought of his missing sword made his temper flare.

"Look out, Riebl!" Merlin yelled from his cell.

Riebl turned, swinging the dagger clumsily. The blade cut through three beings, then another when he drove the blade through its heart. The being crumpled at his feet, a fraction of blackness falling to the side. To Riebl's horror, both the being and the separated piece began to stand again. Riebl spun around, the three he had severed in half turned into six. Slash after slash, for every one Riebl took out, two stood back up to take their places. With sweat trailing down his face, Riebl allowed the dagger to hang from his fingers as clapping resonated around him.

"Ah! This is better than I could've ever imagined!" Kya pushed away from the wall, an eerie smile on her face as she flicked her wrist and all the beings froze where they stood. She walked between them, caressing those that were near, until she stopped in front of Riebl. "All this compliments of the wizard," she informed him while he gasped in breath after ragged breath.

Riebl tried to take a step back, only to be stopped by something solid and strong. He gulped, afraid to move, afraid to even wipe the sweat off his brow.

Kya stepped in close, mere inches from his face. "Thank you," she said. She lifted her hand and twisted it again in the air. Every being melted, to float back to her, melding with her body and the folds of her clothes. Kya swiped her hand in the direction of the cell he had just been in, the door flying open banging against the cell bars.

"Your services are no longer required," she said, as a sneer ran across her lips. With the fling of her hand Riebl felt his body propel into the cell, where he landed on the cold, hard floor in a heap. The dagger Kya had given him clattering to the floor, skidding to a halt under his cement bed.

"Wait here," Rove sent telepathically to Shayne. She turned, standing on the deck as the others headed inside. She waited for him, looking up into his eyes as he took her hands in his and squeezed.

"What are you thinking of doing?" she asked, her voice shaky and fear showing on her pretty face.

Rove squeezed her hands tighter, pulling her closer and touching his forehead to hers. "There's no other way, Shayne," he said as his strong grip kept her from pulling away. "I have to make sure that Rune is safe."

Shayne shook her head, again trying to pull away but she couldn't. "You're going to shift into Rune, aren't you?"

Rove closed his eyes. "Yes, it's the only way." He felt Shayne stiffen and hated that he held her in place. "If Kya gets Rune, she'll open the gateway. I don't know what happens then or why she needs to get there. But I do know it can't be good. We have to stop her."

"How are you going to find her? What if she takes you instead?"

Rove let go of her hands and grabbed her face. He gently lifted it so he could look into her beautiful gray eyes. "I won't do anything until the battle, until absolutely necessary." His heart broke as Shayne's tears fell. "I'll be okay if she takes me. She won't know I'm not Rune, even when she tries to open the gateway and nothing happens."

Shayne closed her eyes, sniffling as she struggled to keep her composer. "You don't want me to tell anyone what you have planned, do you?"

Rove breathed in a deep breath, blinking back his own tears and running a hand down her hair. "No, not even Finn. I may not need to do anything. It all depends on how this plays out." He placed his fingers under her chin and lifted her face to his. He kissed her then, tasting the salt from her tears on her lips. He could feel her sadness when her arms came around his neck and held on tight and he buried his face in her hair.

"I'll be okay," Rove repeated, whispering in her ear. "Don't worry about me. My powers are stronger than hers. I promise you, I'll be okay."

2 8

"Here you go, old man."

Merlin watched as a tray laden with food slid across the floor of his cell and stopped at his feet. He looked up into the black eyes of his captor.

"You might want to nibble on that tray of food," Kya said as she pointed to it with a long black nail. "When I return, I will be too busy to feed you."

Merlin hurriedly went to the bars, his foot hitting the tray and food scattering onto the floor. "Please, Kya, you can't do this," he begged, tears trailing down his cheeks. "They don't know anything about the Enchanted Realm. They can't help you!"

"Oh, but that's where you're wrong." Kya reached in and wiped away a tear from his face. "You see, I received a vision. Your grandson, the one with the white streaks in his hair? He's the key to opening the gateway. I am merely going to retrieve him to do my bidding."

Merlin swallowed hard. "No, Kya. Visions aren't always reliable. You know that! I am the only one who can open the gateway from this dimension. Take me to it! I'll open it!" he lied.

Kya tsked, waging a finger at him and chuckling deep in her throat. "So now you want to help me so you can save your grandson?" Kya threw her black hair behind her shoulder as she turned away. "No worries old man,

I'm not going to hurt him. I'm just going to retrieve him. Soon you'll have a new roommate! Tah Tah!"

Tears of hopelessness left Merlin as he pushed away from the bars. He sobbed, grabbing onto the black bands and pulling with everything he had. He yelled out to anyone who may be listening, begging for help to save his family. But no response came, not even from the nightwalker imprisoned in his own cell, staring at him from across the dungeon.

"STOP SCRATCHING, VLAD," Rove demanded. "You're flaking all over the place. If you would've worn the sunscreen like I told you, this never would've happened."

"Thank you for the reminder of your thoughtfulness. I will keep it in mind next time."

"You know, you kind of look like an old snake that can't keep its skin on anymore."

"Thank you, Rove, for that delightful description I hadn't thought of," Vlad answered sarcastically.

"Maybe we should have Maya conjure some baby oil. We could slather it all over you and throw you right at Kya. She'd go to grab you and you'd pop right out of her grasp."

Rune stood with his hands on his hips staring out across the field of tall grasses and laughed as the conversation continued behind him. It was a beautiful day, not a cloud in the blue sky. It was really too bad they were about to make it ugly. He felt arms encircle him, just as he had known they would, and rested his own on Teagan's.

"Maybe we shouldn't do this," she said.

"We have to," he answered, watching a sand hill crane take flight. "If we don't, we'll never stop her."

She sighed as she squeezed him. "We don't even know how to stop her," Teagan answered in frustration. "She always seems one step ahead of us."

Rune turned in her arms placing his around her neck. "We've come up with a plan. All we can do is wait as it plays out."

"But what if what Shayne saw comes true?"

"You can't go by what ifs. You have to go by what is."

Teagan spun around and Rune conjured an orb into his upturned hand, which he quickly extinguished when he saw who had spoken.

"Posh?" Teagan returned swords back where they had come from to go to her friend. But Posh stepped back, stuffing her hands in her front pockets, her eyes downcast.

"I've been staying in the house," she said, indicating the farmhouse with a jilt of her head. "I couldn't seem to go very far away. Just in case you needed more help."

Teagan stepped forward, trying to grab one of Posh's arms before she could step away and failed. "Look at me, Posh."

Posh toed the ground with her shoe before slowly lifting her head. She looked to Teagan with sadness in her red tinted black eyes.

"Oh, Posh," Teagan said lifting a hand to touch her face. "You shouldn't have left. I know you'd never hurt me."

A smile crept across Posh's face as she lifted a hand and grabbed onto Teagan's arm. "You should be more careful who you keep company with," she said as she threw Teagan across the yard toward the farmhouse where she landed with a sickening crack.

Rune transported, skidding onto the ground next to Teagan. She lifted her head, road rash decorated the side of her face and down one arm which was bent at an odd angle. With a hiss, Teagan conjured her swords into each hand. Whiteness enveloped her, mending her injuries as she got quickly to her feet.

"That's not Posh."

Rune scrambled up calling to the others telepathically, an orb in each hand. He let his fangs descend as Posh turned into something much more evil than the darkest vampire could ever be.

"So that's how you're not dead yet." Darkness swirled as eyes turned to inky blackness, laughter left lips sounding more insane than good. Posh's features turned to evil. Her hair, as black as that floating around her, grew in waves descending farther down her back. Simple black clothes turned into a black dress, where blackness billowed out from under its hem to slither across bare feet.

"Where did she come from?" Rove shouted over wind that howled.

"She was pretending to be Posh," Teagan answered squaring her shoulders. "She could've taken Rune right then and there."

"Why didn't she?" Maya asked as wind and hair whipped into her face.

"What good would that have been?" Kya snarled. "I came to have some fun!" She lifted her hands above her head and clapped them as if she had canastas in her grasp. Blackness shot out from her in all directions and began to grow where they landed. Black beings, more than they were able to count, began to move even before they had legs to walk on.

"Span out!" Roam yelled. "Keep an eye out for Riebl. He has to be here somewhere."

They moved as a unit, two together, as they all widened out to fight. Rune stepped to the side as Teagan spun, taking out the first two black beings. His smile faltered when the slit pieces began to rise again as four.

"Crap!" he yelled, throwing an oversized orb. "We got a major problem here!" His orb exploded in the center of several beings, for each piece that flew, two beings replaced that one small piece.

"Don't let them touch you!" Francesca yelled telepathically, taking to the sky to land on the roof of the barn with Aradney in her arms. *"Aradney has black burns. Don't let them grab onto you!"*

"We have to figure out another plan and fast!" Rune responded, backing up as more advanced and he had no choice but defend himself.

"Everyone not possessing an active power, to the roof as we discussed!" Mom yelled as she joined them and Dad grabbed Shayne to transport her to the roof. *"Maya, get ready with your barrier!"*

"What do we do?" Roam's voice played in his head as a barrier dropped around everyone on the roof. Everyone, except a bat who high-tailed it out before the barrier sealed. *"We'll just make more!"*

"There has to be something we can do," Rove answered, as fire left his fingers to take out the beings closing in on him. *"We can't just stand here and let them take Rune!"*

Rune stared at the charred ground as fire danced and sparked, the beings Rove took out didn't get back up. *"It's fire!"* Rune shouted telepathically, throwing another orb at advancing beings. *"The ones Rove hit didn't get back up!"*

"*Are you sure?*" Dad asked his voice slightly muffled from inside the barrier.

Rove shot from the ground to hover above the beings. He snapped his arms down, and the fire on his ropes became more intense engulfing most of his body. Rune could swear he saw a phoenix flash in the midst of the flames as Rove literally shot out columns of fire from each arm.

"*That's a confirmation!*" Vlad reported, still in bat form and flying in a wide circle.

Rune stole a glance in Kya's direction. She stopped examining her nails and stood from the tree she'd been leaning against, her face a picture of surprise and horror.

"That's not possible!" she screamed. "I did everything right! That's not possible!"

"Obviously it is," Rove retorted with a chuckle, softly landing on the ground next to Rune. "Better luck next time!"

Kya's face turned a nasty shade of red. She lifted her arms from her sides, fingers splayed wide. "We'll see," she responded as blackness shot from her hands and body, unknown words leaving her lips.

"*What is she saying, Shayne?*" Rune sent telepathically as wind howled through spinning mini tornadoes. Inky blackness shot out of their centers all across the ground until all you could see was black. More beings grew, to replace those already taken, and more to fill the area so all you saw was Kya's army.

"*She said; 'Bring them onto me, all my beings twice fold. Bring their weapons forth and do my bidding.'*"

"*That doesn't sound good,*" Roam said as blue lightning shot from his fingers. "*We have to move faster than her! Rove, get back up there and take more out!*"

Rove shot up, only to be slammed off course by a mini tornado. He landed halfway into the field where he took to the sky again and fired. "*I'm okay. She actually did me a favor, less wind here.*"

"*We have to keep her occupied!*" Maya yelled as she encircled several beings inside barriers. "*Keep her attention off of Rove!*"

"*Rune, can you get her attention?*" Teagan asked. "*It's you she wants.*"

"Don't go too far away from any of us," Roam reminded. *"Just draw her attention, that's it."*

"Alright, here it goes." Rune transported backward with Teagan and his mom remaining in front of him, Roam and Maya behind him. He conjured an orb into his right hand and let it grow as large as he could. He watched for any reaction from Kya, putting complete trust into his family to protect him. With a deep breath, Rune transported again to the other side of Roam, turning to face Kya. Her black eyes grew as Rune drew his arm back and let it fly. He had never conjured one this large and was surprised by the tremble of the ground as it hit a few feet in front of Kya. He was pleasantly pleased when the sorceress fell hard to the ground, arms and legs flailing.

"Again, Rune!" Dad yelled.

Rune nodded, transporting to the other side of Teagan as Rove moved closer and shot fire down taking out the beings closest to Kya. Once again, the sorceress was able to move out of harm's way and a streak of swear words resonated in Rune's head. He concentrated, making it as large as the last as something sharp pierced him in his side. Pain radiated as Rune turned, dropping his orb onto a black being whose hand was in the shape of a very large knife. Rune looked down, removing his blood soaked hand from the side he had automatically covered. "He got me," he said as his knees gave way and he fell to the ground.

"No!" Teagan screamed. She jabbed and swung taking out any being near her as she tried desperately to get to Rune. Screams sounded from both Shayne and Maya as Roam and Rove doubled over, their hands on their sides, as they felt Rune's pain before putting up barriers in their minds. A purple barrier shot up around Rune's still form as Teagan fought with everything she had, her muscles protesting in places she hadn't even known existed. She fought with more beings, swords and knives taking the place of hands. She slashed and spun as exhaustion threatened to take over, the being in front of her spitting into two as a streak of fire shot across the ground taking out any near her. She tried to run again toward Rune, only to have more beings grow up from the ground at her feet and she had no choice but to keep fighting.

"It's time. Get to Rune, Teagan. He needs you."

A scream bounced inside her skull as Teagan turned. Rove fired one last time before extinguishing his ropes and sending them away. With eyes darting between fiend and Rove, Teagan watched as red streaked hair turned into white and began running through the beings into Kya's line of vision.

"Time for what?" Roam asked, sending out a powerful stream of lightning. *"Rove? Time for what?"*

"Do something, Teagan!" Shayne cried.

It all happened quickly as no answer came from Rove, only yelling from everyone else and the sobbing of Shayne within their telepathy.

Teagan continued to fight, her body threatening to collapse. A gasp sounded next to her as Adrianna noticed Rove as Rune being surrounded by beings, the white streaks in his hair seeming more noticeable than it should be. Adrianna lifted Excalibur and fought with a vengeance to get to her son, swinging and cutting any being in her path, as she cried out Rune's name, beings reformed and refilled the path she was trying to make.

Teagan swung, decapitating the nearest being, sweat pouring down her back and tears warping her vision. She stole a glance in Kya's direction as a sneer traveled across the sorceress's lips as a bat circled her. She lifted her hand and flung it to the side, Vlad was thrown into a tree twenty feet away. Kya smiled, locking eyes with her as she clapped her hands. All the black beings, except the ones encircling Rove, dropped where they stood to slither across the ground and disappear to their mistress. With a final laugh, Kya's hand latched onto Rove and in a blink, they were gone.

Roam froze where he stood, residual lightning leaving his fingertips, staring where Kya had just been. Adrianna dropped to her knees in grief as shouting and snaps to the air hung in the confusion as those banned to the roof joined their loved ones. Teagan moved, running across the scorched grass toward the real Rune and fell to her knees next to him as the purple barrier vanished.

With a shaking hand, Teagan reached out to touch Rune's lifeless body as her sword became engulfed in whiteness.

Continue this adventure in the final book of this trilogy

A Day Yet To Come

Continue reading for a sneak peek at the first chapter!

THANK YOU FOR READING

Did you enjoy this book?

We invite you to leave a review at the website of your choice, such as Goodreads, Amazon, Barnes & Noble, etc.

DID YOU KNOW THAT LEAVING A REVIEW...

- Helps other readers find books they may enjoy.
- Gives you a chance to let your voice be heard.
- Gives authors recognition for their hard work.
- Doesn't have to be long. A sentence or two about why you liked the book will do.

Don't miss out on your next favorite book!

Join the Melange Books mailing list at
www.melange-books.com/mail.html

Subscriber Perks Include:

- First peeks at upcoming releases.
- Exclusive giveaways.
- News of book sales and freebies right in your inbox.
- And more!

Don't miss
the final book in the
Dark as Night Trilogy

A Day Yet to Come

A FINAL PROPHECY

Before a day without a night, one will shift over to take on the fight.
He will hide his plan from those he loves to take one on, to fight alone.
The sisters three must combine as one, to secure the gateway and make
it sound.
One that sees, and one that binds, the last to protect the one who must hide.
A wish, a prayer, a truth to know. Accept these things, a family once more.

ONE FIGHTS ALONE

Rove Gustavo has a new power and swears his girlfriend to secrecy so he
can save his brother from the evil clutches of the Sorceress Kya. Will his
family understand or will Shayne Adams return home when blame is thrust
upon her?

AN ENCHANTED REALM

Powers grow, love soars and enemies turn friend. Will those who were
chosen before they were born protect a magical realm and keep magic alive,
or will they die trying to protect something they never knew existed?

Chapter One

Grief, like nothing she had ever felt before, dropped her to her knees threatening to break her heart. Voices shouted next to her as hands lifted her from the warm brown roof of the barn to securely land her on the ground near her best friend, Teagan Finnegan. Total pandemonium broke out around her as everyone ran in different directions to the injured, as fresh tears fell from Shayne Adam's eyes making it difficult for her to see.

The once vibrant green grass was now trampled from the battle between good and evil. The Sorceress Kya and her charred black army were gone, leaving behind blackened earth and uprooted ground. Radek Gustavo kneeled by his beloved Francesca with an injured Aradney in her arms; her black burned arms were visible even from where Shayne stood. Roam Gustavo and Maya Stewart knelt next to where Vlad lay lifeless across the Field, just feet from where Rove Gustavo had been grabbed by Kya and taken away. More tears trailed down her face at the thought of the one she loves now gone as Diego, former enemy now friend, ran past her and dropped down next to Teagan.

"Vlad is badly injured," he said with panic, looking down at Rune Gustavo lying lifeless on the ground.

"As soon as I heal Rune I'll be there," Teagan wiped away tears with her shoulder. Her magical Celtic sword's glowing tip touching her right hand where it lay on Rune's gaping wound, his face almost as white as the streaks in his raven hair. "He's mortally wounded. My sword is healing him, I can feel it, but he's healing slowly."

"Rune?" Dimitri Gustavo's surprised voice floated through Shayne's ears and drew her attention away from her heartbreak as he knelt on the ground near his son. "I saw Kya take him, how is he here?"

"Dimitri, where is Rove?" Adrianna Gustavo cried, dropping to the ground near Rune's head. "I don't see him anywhere."

"Kya has Rove," Shayne heard herself answer, her voice sounding hollow to her own ears. She lifted her eyes and watched as Rove's parents turned their surprised gazes to her.

"How can that be?" Adrianna asked, her voice bordering on panic.

"Because Rove has a new power," Shayne answered, tears streaming down her face. "He can shape shift. I never thought this would actually happen."

"Rove can shape shift?" Adrianna questioned in both surprise and anguish. "How? When?"

"The night we unintentionally woke you and Dimitri," Shayne answered, her knees threatening to buckle as she spoke, "Teagan and I had been playing cards in the tree house when Rove joined us shape shifting uncontrollably. He asked us to keep it a secret in case he needed to use it unexpectedly. He came to me last night and told me that if anything went wrong today, he would take Rune's place to save him."

"This should never have been kept a secret," Adrianna protested, looking to her injured son and back to Shayne.

"I'm so sorry, Adrianna," Shayne pleaded, wiping away tears with shaking fingers as she finally looked into Adrianna's troubled face. "I didn't think..."

"No, you didn't think," Adrianna interrupted, her voice rising. "Rune is injured and Rove is in the clutches of someone far more evil than we anticipated. No, Shayne, you didn't think..." her voice trailed off as the ground began to shake under them.

Shayne teetered as the earth shook and trembled. Diego grabbed her arm and drew her to the ground next to him, draping his arm protectively and holding her securely as the ground continued to shake. A white mist appeared to float across the beaten ground, covering it in a sheet of white, until it built in intensity making her shield her eyes from its brightness.

The whiteness diminished as quickly as it had come, bringing the Gustavo living room into focus. Instead of the hard ground, Shayne was now sitting on soft carpeting while Rune was laid out on the couch, Teagan stood beside him her sword split into two, ready to battle whatever was now coming. Maya and Roam stood over an unconscious Vlad lying on the carpet near the doorway to the kitchen, a protective purple barrier surrounding his still form.

"Adrianna, did you do this?" Radek asked from across the room where he stood protectively over Francesca with a sobbing Aradney in her arms, his fangs descended and the color of his eyes red.

"No." She shook her head, Excalibur gleaming in her right hand. "I don't have that kind of power, not without a spell."

"Then who did?" Roam asked with his blue lightning power arcing from his hands as he stood protectively over Vlad.

"You don't need your power, Roam. None of you do." The voice was soft, almost musical as it drifted throughout the room. Stars shimmered near Maya, building in intensity until a figure began to appear. Maya popped out another purple barrier as a woman with long blonde hair loosely braided and thrown over the front of her shoulder, appeared in a white tunic and brown slacks reaching her bare feet. Shayne scrunched her eyebrows as she tried to decipher why this woman looked familiar.

"Mother Brea?" Maya exclaimed, her voice catching as tears pooled into her eyes. She dropped her barrier and went into her birth mother's outstretched arms.

"My beautiful daughters," Brea said, embracing Maya and kissing her on her cheek. Shayne was sure she heard her incorrectly. Brea withdrew from Maya's embrace kneeling next to Vlad, touching him on the shoulder. Whiteness, much like the healing power of Teagan's sword, traveled across his body until he began to stir. Brea rifled his hair and smiled as she stood, going next to Aradney and running a hand down the nightwalkers burns, touching a hand to Aradney's cheek before turning and gliding to Rune, touching him gently on his forehead. "Shayne," she said, looking down at Rune as his eyes began to flutter open. "The book, quickly. You must fetch the book of Light and Dark."

Shayne slowly stood, how did this goddess know her name? Her eyes drifted to Teagan and she froze in place. Her friend was standing stiffly, her eyes riveted on Brea. There was no mistaking the absolute stunned expression on her face.

"Mom?"

Shayne jolted in surprise. A photograph of Teagan and her mother popped into her memory as she stared at her best friend and the mother who had abandoned her so long ago. But how could Teagan's mom be Maya's birth mom? Brea smiled sadly, going to Teagan and lifting her hand to her daughter's face, only to have it slapped away.

"Mom? Did you just say, Mom?" Maya questioned, her face showing absolute shock.

Brea took a step back from Teagan, her eyes showing regret and pain. She looked to Maya and then her eyes settled on Shayne. "I'm so sorry, there isn't time for me to explain, my daughters. We must hurry. Shayne, the book," she urged, motioning to her.

"Oh, no, no, no," Teagan demanded using one of her swords as a pointer. "You will explain now."

"Teagan," Brea said, her voice maternal. "I only have a short while to accomplish all I have come to do. Please let me…"

"I don't care!" Teagan yelled, tears pouring down her face. "You left me! Where were you when Dad died? With my sister, you didn't bother to tell me about?"

"Teagan, please. You have every right to ask these questions," Brea stated hurriedly. "I really don't have much time. Shayne, you must retrieve the book and open it. Open it to the black page, hurry!"

"Why?" Teagan asked, placing her body in front of where the book was tucked away under the coffee table. "Tell us why you need Shayne to find the black page."

"Because her sister, Kya, has embraced black magic," a man's deep familiar voice, with a heavy Irish accent, answered moments before he appeared next to Brea wearing similar clothing, except for the leather boots on his feet. "You must know what has been foretold to stop her."

Shayne's hand covered her mouth to stifle the gasp leaving her lips as she stared at the man she knew as well as Dracula.

"Dad? How…" Teagan's swords vanished as fresh tears left her eyes. Her now empty hands went to her face as sobs overtook her.

Aidan Finnegan looked even more handsome than Shayne had remembered him being. His thick, copper brown hair was longer, reaching well past his shoulder blades, his amber eyes just as kind. His body was still muscular, showing even under his clothing. Shayne watched in awe as he left Brea's side and walked slowly to his daughter, extending his arms toward her in invitation. There was no mistaking the relief he showed when Teagan stepped into his arms and laid her head on his chest. "I know this is hard for you to process, Teagan, and you have every right to be angry with me and with your mom. You have to understand this has all been done for a reason, a reason we cannot yet tell you about. You and your sisters must figure it out on your own."

Shayne stood rigidly. *Aiden just said 'sisters'*, she thought. *We're sisters?*

"Then why are you here?" Teagan asked, her voice muffled by Aidan's shirt. "Why come here at all? So I can watch you leave me again?"

"Aidan, we are almost out of time. We can't stay longer than allowed."

"I know, Brea," Aidan answered. "I haven't seen Maya since she was a wee baby," he said as he turned to look at her and then to Shayne. "Our daughters are beautiful." His voice caught and he ran a hand down Teagan's hair and kissed the top of her head. "As your mother has said, we only have a short time to accomplish this. The longer we stay the better chance of Kya sensing us and then all will be lost. Shayne must go to the book and touch the black page."

Brea went to Maya, hugging her and kissing her on the forehead. "All will be explained soon," Brea said, before going to Shayne and running a hand gently down her face before kissing her cheek. "But be warned and be careful. Kya is deadly."

Brea returned to Aidan, cupping Teagan's chin in her hand. "I have never stopped loving you, any of you." Her bottom lip quivered and a tear rolled down her cheek as she gazed at Teagan's face.

Aiden's eyes roamed the room. "You will find what you seek at Vlad's castle. I'm sorry, that is all we can tell you for now."

"Don't leave me again," Teagan begged grabbing onto her parents. Aidan dried her tears and gently disentangled them both. He moved Teagan to Rune now sitting on the couch and whispered into his ear before stepping away to rejoin Brea, putting his arm around her.

"We won't be far," he said nodding to Vlad as their bodies began to shimmer. "Touch the page, Shayne. Read what it says."

"We will come back to you all," Brea added. "When the moon is high and the sky is bright and answer all your questions, we promise. Light and love to you, my daughters. Blessed be."

The room suddenly felt empty and way too quiet. Shayne slowly knelt on the floor by the coffee table and withdrew the book from underneath with mixed feelings running through her thoughts. She carefully removed the black cloth from around it, camouflaging it from being seen by others, and sat down on the floor with her hand on the book's blank cover. She was Teagan and Maya's sister. She was the daughter of a sorceress. How did she not know?

"What did my dad say to you?" Teagan asked Rune as she sat beside him.

"To take care of you and remind you that we are all in this together."

Shayne glanced at Teagan from the corner of her eye, jealousy seeping into her mind as her hand lay still on the book's cover.

Teagan placed her head on Rune's shoulder. "Open the book, Shayne. We better find out what the black page says."

"We can't open it yet," Rune said looking around the room. "Rove isn't here. Where is he?"

Shayne swallowed nervously and spoke before anyone else could. "Rove took your place, Rune. He's with Kya."

"Excuse me?" Rune responded, his body jerking in her direction while Shayne avoided his eyes. "What do you mean he took my place?"

"Apparently Rove received a new power," Roam answered sitting on the arm of the couch next to his brother. "He was able to shape shift into you and allowed Kya to capture him when you were injured."

"Why? Why would he do that?" Rune questioned. "She's going to kill him!"

"No, she won't," Teagan clarified, placing her hand on his cheek and forcing him to look at her. "As long as Rove looks like you he's safe. She won't know the difference."

"She'll know if he can't open the gateway!"

"She won't be able to open it until the summer solstice," Shayne interjected keeping her eyes on the book. "We have twelve days to get Rove back."

"Did you know, Shayne, that Rove could shape shift?"

Shayne licked her lips nervously, running her hand down the cover of the boy's book. She lifted her tear-filled eyes to look at Rune. "Yes, I knew. I also knew when he was going to take your place. Rove asked me not to say anything."

Rune ran his hand through his hair. "You knew and still you allowed him to take *my* place and be taken by Kya! How could you do that?"

"I didn't have much of a choice, Rune," Shayne answered, slowly getting to her feet and placing the large book on the coffee table. "I don't like this anymore than anyone else." She turned her back on them all and left the room.

It smelled like an old basement and the surface he had just been thrown to felt like one too. Something clanged shut behind him and Rove Gustavo placed his hands on the cold concrete floor, slowly lifting his head. He peered to his left and wasn't too surprised to see bars a short distance away. Slowly, he got into a sitting position and looked around. He was definitely in a cell, and could only hope it was in Merlin's castle.

"Rove! Are you alright?"

Panic tore into him as he scrambled to his feet, grabbed onto the bars and stared into the cell directly across from his. Pappy stood exactly as he was, staring back at him.

"Who did you call me?" he asked unable to keep the panic out of his voice.

"I called you Rove. Did you hit your head? Are you bleeding?"

Rove concentrated, placing a picture of Rune in his mind to turn back into his brother. "Who am I now?"

Pappy stared at him, alarm and confusion showing on his face. "You're still Rove, are you supposed to be someone else?"

Rove backed up, calling to his dragon scaled ropes, but nothing happened. "Why aren't my powers working?"

The voice that responded was quieter, but familiar, coming from the far end of his cell. "Do you have black bands around your wrists?"

Lifting both arms, Rove stared in disbelief at the black bands tied securely around both wrists. He placed his fingers underneath and tugged, but they were held fast. "Pappy, what are these? How do I get these blasted things off?"

"You can't," Pappy answered, sticking his hands out between the bars to show Rove his own black bands.

"Kya conjured them with black magic from her creepy black book."

Rove turned, running to the end of his cell and grabbing onto the bars. He knew that voice. A stream of swear words left his lips when he recognized Riebl sitting on the floor of the cell adjacent to his. "At least you're where you should be!" he snarled.

Riebl picked something up from off the floor of his cell and tossed it through his bars. "Yeah, yeah, yeah, I know, everyone's happy." He placed a hand on the floor and hoisted himself to his feet. "Unfortunately, with me here, there is no escape for either of you. And trust me, that's a bad thing."

"Trust you!" Rove yelled. "You tried to kill my brother you worthless piece of crap!"

"Now, that's the old me," Riebl answered, leaning a shoulder against his bars. "I'll make it up to all of you, that is, if we can get out of here."

A laugh escaped Rove's lips. "I can promise you, if I get out of here you're the last person I would think of helping to escape."

"Rove, I have to know, is everyone okay?" Pappy called.

Rove sneered at Riebl before going back to the door of his cell, placing his hands back onto the bars. "I don't know how everyone is, Pappy. We were battling Kya and her black army, Rune was stabbed and I had no choice but to take his place to save him."

"Rune was stabbed?" Pappy exclaimed alarmed. "How in the world did you think taking his place would save him?"

"Teagan will heal him and he'll be okay, he has to be." Rove placed his forehead on the cold steel of the bars, moments of doubt clouding his mind. He pushed the thoughts aside; he had to assume Rune was fine and right now trying to find a way to get him back from Kya's clutches. He lifted his eyes to Pappy, knowing they showed his concern. "I can shape shift now, Pappy. It just happened one night. I told Shayne that if things went wrong I would shape shift into Rune and let Kya take me. But now she's going to know I'm not Rune. She'll go back once she knows. Pappy, we have to do something or everything I've done will be for nothing."

Pappy sighed, dropping his head down. "It's these bands. They prevent us from using good magic. I can't do anything either with these on."

"What do we do?"

"Pray she doesn't come in here," Riebl responded. "She's totally wacked.

She'll take us all out once she sees your red streaks and not the one she needs."

"I could care less what she does to you," Rove retorted, snarling at the nightwalker before turning back to his grandfather. "Pappy, there has to be a way. What do we do?"

Pappy's eyes stayed riveted to the floor as the ancient wizard slid down to sit on the cold cement. "The only thing we can do, pray."

A Day Yet to Come
Book 2 of the Dark as Night trilogy
is available wherever books are sold.

ABOUT THE AUTHOR

"If, when you wake up in the morning, you can think of nothing but writing...then you are a writer."

— RAINER MARIA RILKE

After hearing this saying in the movie, *Sister Act 2*, it inspired JT Adeline to push herself forward and make her dream a reality. She is the author of *The Dark As Night Trilogy*, and *Unexpected Match Maker* included in the Second Chance for Love Anthology.

JT lives in Minnesota with her husband and two grown sons. If she is not writing, you can usually find her in her art room, spending time with family and friends, or outside with her beloved American Bulldog, Mylo.

Stayed tuned for more exciting adventures coming your way!

You can find JT at Facebook at
www.facebook.com/JTAdeline

ALSO BY JT ADELINE

WITH FIRE & ICE YOUNG ADULT BOOKS

Dark as Night Trilogy

A Day as Dark as Night

A Day Without a Night

A Day Yet to Come

WITH SATIN ROMANCE

Unexpected Match Maker in the Second Chance For Love anthology